MOUNTAIN MAN PROTECTOR

COLE BROTHERS BOOK FOUR

CRYSTAL MONROE

DESCRIPTION

I'll save her. Then I'll make her mine.

I know what they think of me in this small town.
Broken from the Marines. Dangerous.
That reputation suits me just fine.
I swore long ago I'd never get close to anyone again.

But then a city girl shows up on my mountain.
Audrey's on the run, hiding from her abusive ex-boyfriend.
Her wide-eyed innocence wakes the savage beast I'd locked
away.

I'll wage war to keep Audrey safe.
Her stalker ex will regret the day he set foot in my town.
And when I'm done, I'll claim her as mine.

But is my dark secret the biggest threat of all?

*Mountain Man Protector is a standalone, full-length
romance with no cheating or cliffhangers.*

The books in the Cole Brothers series can be read in any order.

ONE
AUDREY

New life. A fresh start.
The words came to me as I jogged along the path.

The small town I'd moved to really *was* a fresh start. I was grateful. And this forest trail just outside of town was perfect.

Then I saw something that made me come to a skidding halt.

A boot print in the mud.

My heart froze in my chest.

Slowly, I got closer to examine it. The print was huge.

Only Wayne, well over six feet and weighing 200 pounds, had boots that large.

I tensed, gasping for breath.

Oh my God. He's found me!

I looked around the quiet woods. A million questions flooded my mind at once.

How had my insane ex-boyfriend discovered my hiding place? Had he followed me all the way to this little town in Virginia?

Was he out here now, watching me from the shadows?

In the near distance, a twig snapped. A bush rustled.

He was after me!

I broke into a sprint, running as fast as I could through the forest. I had to put as much distance between me and Wayne as possible.

Alone here in the wilderness, with no one to stop him, he would surely carry out his threat to kill me.

I *had* to escape. My life depended on it.

Tearing through the woods, I dodged branches and rocks. Not wasting time to look over my shoulder, I pushed myself forward, flying through the forest at my maximum speed.

At any moment, I expected him to grab me, his huge hands wrapping around my shoulders and pulling me to a stop.

I ran until I thought my heart would explode.

After what felt like forever, my lungs were on fire. I gasped for air.

Unable to run another step, I staggered to a stop. Bent forward with my hands on my knees, I struggled to catch my breath.

Despite my fear, Wayne didn't appear. There was no sound of anyone following me anymore.

I must have outrun him.

I could hardly believe it. I had escaped Wayne yet again.

Relief flowed through me, but I knew I couldn't stay in one place for long. He was probably still out there, searching for me.

I gulped air in deep breaths.

Calm. Must stay calm to plan your next move.

As I regained my composure, I took in my surroundings. The forest was thicker here. Nothing was familiar.

How far had I run? Where was the path I'd been following?

I grimaced. In my panic, I had run off the trail, and now it was nowhere to be seen.

Without any landmarks, I was lost in the woods.

My stomach twisted in fear.

The sun had set during my frenzied run, throwing the woods deeper into darkness by the minute. The fading light made it even harder to get my bearings.

I kicked myself for leaving my cell phone at home.

It's okay. Just don't panic.

As a biology teacher, I knew how fragile the human body was, and how easy it would be to die of exposure – not to mention the animals and other dangers that lived in the forest.

I set off toward the direction I'd come from, confident I'd spot the trail quickly. But as I moved through the woods, I found nothing but a thick tangle of underbrush and trees.

Soon the forest was totally dark, and I was no longer sure which direction was home.

This is not good, Audrey. Not good at all.

My throat closed up and my palms grew sweaty despite the rapidly dropping temperatures. Ignoring the fear mounting inside me, I continued onward.

Everything's okay. I'll find a path eventually.

I tried to stop the panic from consuming me, but my breath caught in my lungs. The dark night seemed to close in around me.

Not only was I lost, but my stalker ex was probably out here somewhere, just waiting for me.

The only thing working in my favor was the moon,

which was shining full and bright as it rose in the star-filled sky.

I picked my way through the forest, careful not to trip on any large tree roots or protruding rocks.

The last thing I needed was a twisted ankle.

Suddenly, I caught a whiff of wood smoke in the air, and my heart filled with hope.

Someone must have been burning a fire nearby. Following the scent, I was rewarded with the sight of a cabin in the distance.

Thank God! I'm not going to die out here.

The knot in my stomach loosened as I caught sight of firelight glowing happily through the cabin windows. I rushed forward into the clearing with a huge sense of relief.

That was when I ran smack into what felt like a brick wall.

"What are you doing on my property?"

The unfamiliar man towered over me in the moonlight.

He was huge—even bigger than Wayne. He must have stood over six foot four, with massive shoulders, cropped brown hair, deep blue eyes, and a short beard.

He was positively rippling with muscles, and several tattoos on his arms and chest peeked out from his shirt. His look screamed sexy lumberjack, with his red flannel shirt, jeans, and sturdy work boots.

As I looked down at his boots, I noticed the prints in the dirt around where he stood matched the print in the mud from the jogging trail.

Oh, crap!

Wayne wasn't stalking me after all. The prints had come from this handsome stranger living in a log cabin deep in the forest.

Relief mixed with deep embarrassment flooded through

me, and I didn't know if I should laugh or cry at my own stupid paranoia.

The stranger looked at me with suspicion.

"What the *hell* are you doing on my property?" he demanded again. His voice was deep and sonorous, and he smelled like pine needles and fresh-cut wood.

"I'm Audrey Sawyer." I stammered for a moment, but as I kept talking my voice grew more sure. "I'm renting a cottage at the edge of town. I was jogging through the woods just before sunset, and ..." I trailed off. I didn't want to mention the panic attack sparked by fear of my violent ex-boyfriend. "I lost the trail and didn't know the way back home. Then I saw the light from your cabin."

He gave a quick nod, seeming to believe my story. He looked me up and down, as if appraising me and my designer workout clothes.

"You're not from around here, are you?"

"No, I just moved to North Haven a few weeks ago."

"Typical. City folks should stay out of the woods. Especially at night."

He turned his back to me and strode to a tree stump with an ax buried in it. A pile of logs was stacked next to it, and he picked one up, set it on the stump, and swung the ax to split the log in half.

His muscles tensed as he bent over to retrieve the two pieces, and I felt a longing deep inside me that I hadn't felt in ages.

"So? Can you help me find the trail back home?" I asked hesitantly.

He shook his head stoically. "You'll just get lost again if you go out there looking for it, city girl. Go inside my cabin. Get warm by the fire. I'll drive you home as soon as I finish this."

I nodded, but paused before I followed his orders. He was a stranger, after all.

"I don't even know your name," I said.

"Noah Cole. Now go inside and get out of the cold. The temperature in the forest drops fast once the sun sets, and you're not properly dressed for it."

"I'm wearing running gear," I said defensively.

"Well, you're not on a treadmill in a fancy city gym," he replied. "You need to keep your core temperature up, and that fancy label isn't gonna do it. Now, quit arguing and go inside."

He had an imposing presence with his bulky frame and take-charge attitude. But I wasn't afraid.

Living in fear of Wayne had honed my gut instinct about men, and I could tell Noah had my best interest at heart.

In a weird way, it was almost sweet how he was being protective of me. Plus, a fire sounded amazing. I walked up the steps of the cabin and went inside.

The interior of the cabin was sparse but cozy. I stood by the wood stove and warmed my freezing hands. The fear that had coursed through my veins moments before melted away.

I was going to be all right. Wayne didn't know my location, and I'd soon be back at my cottage, thanks to the hot lumberjack outside.

I was safe.

Near the stove, there was a chair of exquisitely hand-crafted wood with a hand-knit blanket draped over it. Everything was tidy and ordered.

On the wall were pictures of servicemen and framed medals. Mr. Sexy Lumberjack was a former Marine.

Interesting.

Even more interesting was that I saw no signs of a woman living with him. This was a bachelor pad, for sure. He clearly lived alone.

And he's hot as hell.

I cringed at what he must have thought of me. I'd gotten lost in the woods like a fool, but I'd had good reason to get spooked.

It was only normal after the nightmare I'd just escaped.

Just six months before, I'd been living in a luxury apartment in Charlotte, North Carolina, with my boyfriend Wayne Thornton.

When we first met, I thought he was my Prince Charming. He was successful and witty, and he treated me well for a while. But he quickly revealed himself to be controlling and abusive.

When he proposed to me on my twenty-fifth birthday, I declined and told him I wanted to break up instead.

Wayne refused to accept that I didn't love him anymore, and he kept insisting that we were meant to be together forever. He stalked me at the private school where I worked, and at my parents' house where I went back to stay in my old bedroom.

He followed me everywhere I went, confronting me in stores and slashing my tires when I refused to get back together with him. He violated restraining orders.

I was scared out of my mind.

Finally, Wayne left a terrifying message on my phone.

If I didn't accept his proposal, he said, he'd kill me.

That was my breaking point.

I fled North Carolina in the middle of the night, picking my destination at random. I'd have done anything to escape his violent temper.

I ended up in the little isolated town of North Haven. It

was a different world from Charlotte, and I knew there was no way Wayne would ever look for me in an itty-bitty village in the Blue Ridge Mountains of Southern Virginia.

It was the start of a new life.

Luck had been on my side. I'd gotten a job as a biology teacher at the local middle school, and used the cash I'd saved up to pay the deposits on an adorable little rental house just on the outskirts of town, nestled at the base of the forest. It was like a gingerbread cottage, and I felt like I was living in a fairy tale every time I walked up the cobblestone path to come home after work.

When I'd gone for a jog that afternoon, the colors of the foliage in the dimming light were breathtakingly beautiful.

This is why I love living in the country, I'd thought as I set out on the trail.

I'd never expected to feel that way. I'd always thought of myself as a city girl. Born and bred in Charlotte, I'd lived for the nightlife, art museums, and buzz of the city. But I'd already fallen in love with my new home.

The townsfolk in North Haven were friendly and welcomed me into their fold with open arms. It was the kind of place where neighbors watched out for one another. I felt safe and hidden in the tucked-away little town.

But this particular local—Noah Cole—was a little less friendly. Still, though, I sensed I could trust him. In fact, I found him intriguing.

In the distance, I could hear the steady sound of him chopping the logs into firewood. It didn't take long for the sound to stop, and a moment later he entered the cabin with his bulging arms full of logs.

I stepped out of the way as he stacked them by the woodstove.

Finally, he stood next to me, face to face.

I felt the heat coming off his body and his breath on my skin.

"Ready to go?" he asked in that deep, sexy voice of his.

I looked in his intense blue eyes, and the air between us seemed to crackle with electricity. My body suddenly longed to be touched by those strong hands.

I'd never been more attracted to anyone in my life.

Purely on impulse, as if possessed, I leaned forward until my breasts were pressed against his hard chest. I reached out and touched his face, caressing the coarse hairs of his dark beard.

"Only if you're ready for me to leave."

His eyes roamed down to my lips, my neck, and my chest. My heart pounded in anticipation as I wondered what it would be like to kiss this mysterious, sexy Marine living as a mountain man deep in the woods.

My lips parted. I turned my face toward his, ready to be kissed passionately.

Suddenly he stepped back, widening the distance between us as if repulsed.

"Let's go, then," he said and turned toward the front door.

My heart fell. Here I was, practically throwing myself at him, and he'd swiftly rejected me. Such brazen flirtatiousness was unusual for me, but it had clearly not made an impression on Noah.

We both sat in silence as he drove his truck down the bumpy dirt roads toward town. I'd never been so humiliated, and my cheeks burned. He must have thought I was some kind of hideous troll. I couldn't wait to get back to the comfort and safety of my cottage.

"Thanks for the ride," I said as he dropped me off outside my front door, my tone sharp with sarcasm.

"Stick to the trails from now on, city girl," Noah said. "And get some proper clothes. You're not in some fashion photo shoot out here. A proper vest could make the difference between life and death in the real world."

Then he drove away, leaving me baffled and annoyed.

He may have been the sexiest man in all of Virginia, but he was also a complete jackass. I just hoped this was the last time I'd ever have to see him.

TWO
NOAH

"Noah, where are you?"

My business partner's voice came through my cell phone sounding nervous and half panicked. I would have been worried something was wrong, but Sean always sounded that way.

"I'm on my way," I said briskly and hung up my cell. I should have left ten minutes ago, but I was having a hard time staying focused.

No matter how hard I tried not to think about her, my thoughts kept drifting to that sexy damsel in distress I had to drive home last night.

Audrey Sawyer, she'd said her name was. Fuck, she was hot with those full, round tits crammed into that tight little exercise top. She had a tiny waist, and a firm ass, all wrapped up in a sleek designer outfit that accentuated every curve. When she pressed her body against mine, and put her soft hands on my beard, all I wanted to do was kiss that hot mouth, bend her over, and fuck the hell out of her until she came.

That would have been wrong, though.

Bad things happened to everyone I ever got close to, so I'd learned the best thing I could do was keep to myself. If I never cared for anyone, then fate wouldn't take them away. Sure, it made for some lonely nights, but that was a hell of a lot better than the heartbreak of losing someone.

The problem was, knowing Audrey was living so close by, just right at the edge of town, made it a little too tempting to try to see her again. So, I had to make sure she wouldn't want anything to do with me. I felt like an asshole being rude to her, but in the long run it was the kindest thing I could do for her. Too much bad shit was happening in this world, and I'd already seen more than my fair share of it.

I was feeling on edge as I pulled into the parking lot of the hardware store where I was supposed to meet my business partner, Sean Rutherford. He knew I hated coming into town, but he insisted this time it was unavoidable.

I used my mirrors and peripheral vision to carefully check the parking lot before getting out of my truck. I knew there weren't any enemy combatants perched with sniper rifles at Jones Hardware, but old habits die hard.

The last time I failed to properly check for an ambush, a lot of good men died. Hell, they were barely more than boys.

I could feel the hairs on the back of my neck prickle as I walked into the store. The shitty little bell on the door rang, and I felt myself jump. Fuck! I hated looking like a goddamn fool in public like that. Now everybody was staring at me. I turned down the first aisle.

"That's Noah Cole," I heard a lady whisper at the other end of the aisle. "He's the fourth son of Robert Cole."

"The one who's a baseball player?" the woman she was talking to said with a confused look.

"No, the ballplayer is their youngest son, Jared. Noah's a year older than Jared, which makes him about twenty-eight, I think. But he's never been around. He joined the service and when he came back he was a total mess. Now he hides in the woods like some crazy hermit mountain man."

"That's so sad. What branch did he serve in?"

I turned and looked at the gossips pointedly, with a pissed-off glare that made them both jump. "I'm a Marine. Anything else you want to know, why don't you ask me to my face?"

The two women turned bright pink and fled from the aisle. Shit, I hated coming into town. I couldn't stand the residents of North Haven any more than they tolerated me, and that included all four of my brothers, none of whom I'd spent any more time with than I absolutely had to since I got back from Afghanistan.

I trudged down the aisles until I found Sean.

"Noah!" He called me over to the customer service counter with a wave.

"What's so important I had to come here myself?" I growled, but Sean didn't cower.

We'd known each other our whole lives, but we didn't start out as friends. He'd always been scrawny and kinda nerdy, playing Dungeons & Dragons and competing in the Mathlete games, whatever the hell that shit was.

I always hung out with the jocks, playing football, basketball, baseball, or whatever sport was in season at the time. I'd been blessed with strength, speed, and coordination, and I'd used them to my advantage whenever I could.

My family name came with a reputation for being spoiled and greedy, and I was determined to prove that I'd earned my accomplishments with hard work, skill, and effort. I practiced sports for hours before and after school every day, and even more on weekends. I wanted to be the best, and that meant winning with honor and integrity. That's why it pissed me off so damn much when I saw those other jocks picking on Sean.

The little guy was clearly out of his league with them in both weight and skill. Shoving him around wasn't a show of strength, it was just flat-out bullying a weaker kid, and that didn't sit well with me.

I got benched for the rest of the season for beating the shit out of three of my fellow teammates, but it was worth it. After that, nobody picked on Sean Rutherford ever again. Sean started sitting at my table every day during lunch, and I was surprised at just how smart he was when it came to numbers and business. I passed calculus and economics because of his help, and I never forgot the favor.

When I got out of the Marines and settled back home in North Haven, Sean was the only guy from high school to look me up. We talked for hours, and for once I didn't feel uncomfortable. I shared with him my ideas of becoming a wilderness guide—leading trips around the mountains surrounding North Haven—and he explained to me the ways I could turn my passion into a real business. He became my partner with a handshake that afternoon.

Sean reached up and tried to clasp me on the shoulder, and said, "They won't open an account for Pine Creek Lodge because some of your documents say Cole Lodge. I thought maybe you could vouch to them that you'll cover all expenses should the business fail. You definitely have the credit score."

The store manager sighed heavily and said, "It's not a question of credit score. This document says Cole Lodge, but that one says Pine Creek Lodge. We don't open accounts for businesses with this kind of suspicious incon-sistency."

"You mean you don't open accounts for businesses run by a Cole." I slammed my fist on the counter a little harder than I meant to. The prejudice folks in this town had against my family name pissed me off. That was exactly why I'd decided at the last minute to call my busi-ness Pine Creek Lodge and not Cole Lodge, but I fucked up some of the paperwork. That's why I needed a partner like Sean to straighten it all out, but that was going to take some time. We needed supplies from the hardware store now.

"It's all right," Sean said calmly. "I'm sure we can find a way to work this out."

"You work it out," I snapped. I was trying to control my temper, but it wasn't working. "I'm fucking leaving."

I stormed out the store, with Sean scrambling behind me.

"We can fix this, but not if you lose your temper or bite everyone's head off," Sean said as I charged through the door and out into the blinding sunlight.

"I don't give a shit!" I snapped, and suddenly I saw her, exiting the bakery next to the hardware store. My brother Owen always brought his kid, Maisy, there for a cookie, but I forgot it was even there.

Shit! It figured the one person I was trying to avoid would be coming out of the business next door right at that moment.

She looked even hotter in the full light of day, wearing a pretty little dress that showed off her long, sexy legs. Her long, rich brown hair was down loose and flowed around her in gentle waves like the mane on a wild mare, and I was eager to run my hands through it and kiss those full pink lips. Luckily, she hadn't seen me, and I figured I could just slip away in my truck and avoid her completely.

"Hey, Audrey!" Sean suddenly called out beside me and waved his arm high in the air.

My throat tightened. How the fuck did he know her?

"Hi, Sean!" Audrey came over with a smile, but her expression darkened when she suddenly noticed me standing beside him.

"I'd like you to meet my business partner, Noah Cole. This is Audrey Sawyer. She's the new biology teacher in town, and we were discussing ways Pine Creek Lodge might be able to offer learning opportunities for her students."

"I hope you mean guided field trips," I said snidely. "Because folks can get lost in those woods pretty easily, especially when they don't know what the hell they're doing."

"My students won't get lost." Audrey's brown eyes sparked indignantly.

"Yeah, right. Because their teacher knows her way around the woods so well?"

Audrey's eyes narrowed. She looked like she was about to tear into me when Sean cut in, looking completely baffled.

"Do you two know each other?" Sean asked, giving me a pointed stare.

Looking Audrey up and down, I smirked and said, "Yeah, we've met."

THREE
AUDREY

There was one major problem with small towns. If you were trying to avoid someone, you were guaranteed to see them everywhere.

I'd been having a great Saturday, exploring the cute downtown shops.

And then I'd run into *him*.

The way he'd looked me up and down with a damned *smirk* on his face made my blood boil. The nerve of that big, ax-wielding blockhead!

I made up an excuse and left, returning to the sanctity of my home. And for my afternoon jog, I set out in the opposite direction from his cabin, making sure to leave well before sunset and stick to the trail.

Three days later, I was still fuming about that condescending horse's ass. There was something about Noah Cole that was infuriating! He was so smug in his dismissal of me as a city girl who couldn't find her way through the woods.

But I was an expert hiker and had done mountain climbing on weekends in college. Plus, I had a degree in education with a specialty in biology and earth sciences. I could identify countless plant and animal species, more than he could for sure, the stupid muscle-bound hermit!

I sighed as I gathered my things in my classroom at the middle school. I'd spent the day trying to teach a bunch of giggling seventh graders about asexual reproduction, and I was ready to get home and go for a run. There was nothing more challenging than trying to keep a straight face when I knew all my students were mocking the text, and a relaxing jog through the woods near my new home was just what I needed to unwind.

"All right, you're coming with me," a familiar voice called out, and I looked up from my desk to see one of my favorite coworkers standing in the doorway.

Her name was Elisa, and she taught seventh grade algebra in the classroom next to mine. She bounded into my room with her red curls bouncing all around her and a sparkle of mischief in her green eyes.

"Where are we going?" I asked with curiosity.

"It doesn't matter." Elisa grinned as she closed my laptop and shoved my purse and coat at me. "I've known you since the day you came to work here, and in all those weeks, the only thing I've seen you do is work. It's time you joined us for girls' night at the Tavern."

"What's that?" I asked as she grabbed me by the arm gleefully and led me to her car, where two more of our coworkers were waiting.

Lauren taught world history and was recently divorced. I'd heard Elisa teasing her about it in the teachers' lounge on more than one occasion, calling her a cougar because of her sexy, short hairstyle, and the even sexier, shorter dresses she wore outside of work. The other passenger was Bethany. She taught English and was younger and shyer than the other two, often hiding behind her long, dark bangs. Sometimes she reminded me more of a student than a teacher, but the kids responded well to her, which was more than I could say for my teaching style sometimes.

"Hey, girls, Audrey wants to know what the Tavern is!" Elisa called out playfully, and the other two squealed like a couple of tweens at a slumber party.

"It's only the best bar in North Haven, with the hottest bartender!" Lauren exclaimed.

"If you're into that kinda thing." Bethany rolled her big dark eyes.

Lauren licked her lips and said, "Tim Holland serving up drinks, with his rugged good looks, sandy blond hair, and deep blue eyes. Hell, yes, he puts the happy in happy hour!"

"I don't know." Bethany wouldn't sway her opinion. "He's too cocky for me, always running around with one of the Cole brothers, and I hear his parents are a couple of crazy chicken farmers."

The girls all giggled, but when we got to the bar, I had to side with Bethany. The bartender was good-looking, but nowhere near as hot as Noah Cole had been swinging that ax in the moonlight.

Damn it!

Why couldn't I get him out of my mind? Maybe it was because I'd been working too hard. It was time to throw myself into girls' night, I decided. I ordered a round of margaritas for me and the girls and Tim brought them to our table, giving Lauren a chance to blatantly ogle him while Bethany rolled her eyes.

"All right, we want to hear the scoop on life in the big city," Elisa said, and all three girls turned their eyes on me with intense curiosity. "What was it like to live in a big city like Charlotte?"

"What do you want to know?" I flushed, unused to being the center of attention.

"Tell us about the culture and the restaurants," Bethany said. "Have you been to the Bechtler Museum of Modern Art?"

"Did you ride the train there? Are the crowds as crazy as they seem?" Elisa asked.

"No, tell us about the men!" Lauren demanded. "Did you have a boyfriend? Did you have more than one?"

The questions came at me rapid-fire, and I felt like a mini celebrity as I did my best to answer them all as we downed our margaritas.

"The one thing I can say for certain is I'd much rather be right here in peaceful North Haven, where you can actually see the stars at night and everyone knows you by name," I summed up, feeling philosophical as well as slightly tipsy after finishing our second round of drinks.

"Ugh, but it's so boring here and there is absolutely no selection in men," Lauren sighed with exasperation.

"I don't know about that," I said, already feeling comfortable enough in our friendship to challenge her, or maybe it was just the drinks talking. Jerking my thumb back at the bartender, I said, "You did mention liking a certain someone earlier. Is he seeing anyone?"

"Only if you count his best friend, Owen Cole. Those two used to be joined at the hip until they exchanged blows one night down at the Howling Wolf," Elisa said in a conspiratorial whisper that made everyone lean in closer to hear more.

"Leave it to the Cole brothers to stir up trouble," Lauren agreed, piquing my curiosity.

"What's the deal with them?" I tried not to sound too eager, but I had to know.

"Their parents, Robert and Maggie Cole, rolled into town a long time ago when it was little more than dirt," Lauren began. "They were from DC, I think."

"Like forty years ago, before their five sons were born," Bethany added.

"Robert Cole developed North Haven and turned it into a tourist town," Lauren continued. "Built hotels and filled them with tourists. He financed over half the businesses and buildings that now make up North Haven, and he wasn't afraid to cut a dirty deal to do it. A lot of folks lost money through loopholes and tricky contracts. After that, Robert Cole was able to set the wages and the rents. He basically controlled the whole town and he wasn't very nice about it. When he and his wife were killed by a drunk driver about twelve years ago, nobody really shed a tear, except his five sons that he left behind."

"A lot of folks around here are wary of the Cole brothers because their father was such a greedy asshole, but I don't think that's giving them a fair shake," Elisa added her opinion and Bethany nodded in agreement.

"Yeah, when my mom had a stroke, Owen Cole built a ramp to the front door of the house for less than half the cost other contractors were bidding," Bethany said. "I swear, I think he did the labor for free and just charged the cost of the wood. And I've heard he's done a lot of other acts of charity around town too, for folks who don't have a lot of money."

"Same with Dr. Ethan Cole," Elisa said excitedly, making her red curls bob around her face again. "He was extremely nice to me that time I had to go to the ER with a broken arm. Plus, I heard he's performed some expensive surgeries for patients with money from his own pocket."

"So one's a doctor and one's a contractor?" I was trying

to keep it all straight in my head, and the margaritas weren't helping.

"Ethan is the oldest, he's the doctor. Then Gavin, Owen, Noah, and Jared. They've all tried to make a better name for themselves in this town—except for Noah. He'd rather live like a wild man in the woods than work hard to help the community."

"I don't know about that. Noah Cole looks like he works pretty hard to me," I said, thinking of those bulging biceps. A man didn't get a physique like that without a lot of effort.

The women all laughed and gasped. "You've met Noah?"

"I ran into him, twice. The first time while jogging in the woods behind my house, and the second time running errands around town."

"Noah was in town?" Elisa frowned. "That's a rare sighting, like spotting a whale or a unicorn."

Bethany giggled and said, "More like a sexy lumberjack."

"He *does* look like a sexy lumberjack!" Lauren echoed, and I was relieved to know I wasn't the only one who thought that about him.

"Well, sexy or not, stay away from him," Elisa warned me with a wag of her finger. "Of all the Cole Brothers, Noah's the most unpredictable."

"I thought he was a decorated Marine," I said, thinking of the medals I'd seen in his cabin.

"He would have been if he hadn't been dishonorably discharged," Elisa said with a scandalous look in her eye.

"That's a vicious rumor with no truth to it," Lauren chastised her. "I have it on good authority that he was given an honorable discharge after being sent home injured."

"Injured? What happened?" I tried to sound casual.

"He was deployed in Afghanistan when his whole platoon was ambushed," Lauren said, seemingly an endless source of information. "Noah managed to drag two men to safety, but a lot of the others were killed."

"Wow," I said, shaking my head sadly. Noah had been through a lot.

"Apparently, it really impacted him, and he was diagnosed with PTSD," Lauren continued. "It's a good thing he inherited all that money from his father, because I heard he'd never be able to work again, at least not in a job where he'd have to work with the public. He could go off at any time. I feel for the guy, but he's dangerous."

"That's bullshit!" Bethany said. "The war didn't make Noah crazy. He was dangerous before he joined the Marine Corps. Remember that fight he got into at the Howling Wolf?"

"So what? Everybody gets in a fight at that seedy dive. It's what it's known for," Lauren said dismissively.

"Well, Noah Cole used to go there every night before he enlisted," Bethany said. "One night, he nearly beat a man to death."

"Oh please, that was TJ Wilkins, and he had it coming. He makes that story sound worse every time he retells it." Elisa waved her off.

"So you think Noah's not so bad?" I asked lightly, hoping they couldn't see just how interested in him I really was.

"Oh, no. He's a bad boy, all right. Avoid him at all costs," Elisa insisted, looking me right in the eye.

"She's right. Avoid him." Bethany and Lauren both nodded their heads vigorously. It was the one thing my three new friends agreed on, only I still didn't know what to think.

Sure, Noah had been a jerk to me, but now that I knew more about his life, I felt a lot more empathy and compassion for him about it. There was something in his eyes that drew me to him, and I got the feeling he was genuinely concerned for my well-being, almost like a guardian angel, if they came shaped liked sexy mountain men.

My new friends were all convinced he was dangerous, but I wasn't sure what to believe.

For reasons I couldn't explain, I sensed that if I ever needed protection, Noah Cole would be the one I could turn to.

FOUR
NOAH

My adrenaline was pumping as we moved through the small village, clearing one building at a time.

The enemy combatants were holed up in one of them, but there was no way to know which one. It was dangerous work, and everyone was jumpy as hell.

The sand blowing in the wind burned my eyes and chapped my skin, but I ignored it. Suddenly, several rounds of gunfire rang through the air, and we all froze. I looked around in every direction, trying to determine where it had come from, praying to God that one of my men hadn't been hit.

It was my first assignment as a gunnery sergeant, and I had forty-two young men under my command. Shit, most of them were just boys, barely eighteen years old, like I'd been back when I signed up eight years before. They should have been home playing video games, not risking their lives in some town in the middle of Afghanistan.

Yet here they were, trusting their lives to me. I just prayed they hadn't made a huge fucking mistake.

"Sorry! That was me!" Private First Class Lewis called

out, looking utterly humiliated for accidentally discharging his weapon. I couldn't blame the kid for having an itchy trigger finger. We were all scared, and every leaf rustling in the wind had us ready to dive for cover.

I gave the signal to enter the next building, and my men bravely obeyed the command. I could hear shouting and the sound of slamming doors, nothing unusual for a search of this type.

Then suddenly, gunfire—and lots of it.

I called into my radio, trying to find out what was going on, but all I heard back was, "Men down! He's getting away!"

Shit! If someone had shot my men, they sure as hell weren't going to escape while I was there to stop them. With my heart pounding, I charged inside. I ran past my bleeding men where they lay on the floor, crying for their mothers, and rushed toward the open doorway at the end of the hall. That's where he was! That's where he had fled.

I moved cautiously through the doorway and into the room. It was empty, except for the enemy shielding himself behind a hostage. He turned into the light and I could see who he was holding captive. Her brown hair was pulled back in a long braid that hung over her shoulder, and her big brown eyes were wide with fear.

It was Audrey Sawyer! But that was impossible!

I realized in that moment that I was trapped in the middle of nightmare, but I was unable to wake myself from it. All I could do was stand there, frozen, as the enemy pressed his pistol to Audrey's temple. Her face was so beautiful, even when contorted with fear, but there was a determination in her eyes that refused to be defeated. It was the same look she'd given me when I was giving her shit for being lost in the woods, and it made me like and respect her, even as I felt an overwhelming need to protect her.

"Let me go, or her blood will be a stain on your soul forever," the enemy in my dream said.

I set my gun on the dust-covered floor and raised my hands in the surrender position. My pulse was rushing in my ears, and everything seemed to be moving in slow motion. The enemy moved his gun from Audrey's temple and aimed it at me instead. Bravely, Audrey kicked him hard in the kneecap then elbowed him in the stomach. I knew she was tough!

I took advantage of the moment of distraction to charge at him, but I wasn't fast enough. He turned the gun and shot Audrey right in the chest, then escaped out the window.

I ran forward and caught Audrey in my arms. She was soaked in her own blood. Although I barely knew her, my heart was breaking. Such a senseless loss of life. She was so young and had so many great things ahead of her, like falling in love and getting married. Somehow, I had hoped she'd experience those things with me.

"I trusted you to protect me," Audrey whispered in my arms, and then she was dead.

I woke from the nightmare with a shout, sitting bolt upright in bed, drenched in my own sweat.

It took me a moment to realize I was at home in my cabin, safe in my bed. I looked down at my hands to see if they were covered with blood, but of course they were clean. I stumbled to the bathroom on shaky legs and gripped the sink for support while I turned on the water. I splashed some on my face, trying to shake off the panic and heartbreak I was feeling.

It was just a dream. Just a stupid fucking dream!

I was used to the nightmares. I'd been having them

since I came back home over a year ago, but this one was different. Why on earth Audrey had appeared in the dream was at first a mystery, but then the answer came to me.

It was a warning from my subconscious.

Don't let her get close to you.

I was better off alone, and so was everyone who knew me.

I'd never been close to my father—none of us were. He'd been a distant son of a bitch to all his sons. Our mother, however, had always been doting and loving. She spoiled me most of all, because she considered me her miracle baby, and I ate it up. Apparently she'd had a difficult pregnancy with me, and I'd nearly died during childbirth. The doctors said it was a miracle I survived those first few days in the neonatal intensive care unit, and Mom never forgot. She lavished all sorts of extra attention and praise on me, and there was nothing I'd enjoyed more as a kid than rubbing it in my brothers' faces.

But then it had been my fault my parents had died.

I was sixteen, growing like a weed, and constantly hungry. One evening, my parents went to a business meeting downtown. But instead of coming home after, they drove across town to my favorite restaurant. I'd asked my mom to get me a slice of cheesecake, and of course she'd agreed.

That was what killed them.

The police report said their car was preparing to turn left into the restaurant parking lot when it was hit head-on by a drunk driver going the opposite direction.

The guilt nearly destroyed me.

My brothers had insisted that my request didn't make the accident my fault. They said the drunk driver was to blame, but I knew the truth. If it hadn't been for me and my selfishness, our parents would still be alive.

It was a guilt I'd tried to outrun on the ballfield and by playing sports, but try as I might, it was always there. It made a red-hot anger build up inside me.

I was mad at the world, mad at the drunk driver, and in some twisted way, mad at my parents and my brothers. But most of all, I was furious with myself. I hated myself for being responsible for killing two people who had made a huge impact in all our lives.

The town of North Haven seemed to rejoice over their deaths, or at least the death of my father, and that made me angry at them, too. Yeah, my dad hadn't been the nicest man in the world, but his business had done some good in this town, too.

But what worried me was that his blood ran in my veins. If he was a monster that everyone hated, what did that make me? Was I a monster too, just like my father, or was I a hero for having killed him?

Well, I didn't want to be a hero for a fucked-up thing like that, and I was more than willing to punch the shit out of any guy who talked smack about my father.

It got me in a lot of trouble at school, at home, and most especially with the law.

"You're going to be eighteen in a few months, Noah," my grandma had lectured me. "Then you'll be a legal adult. Assault charges won't mean a little suspension from school, they'll mean jail time. You'd better wise up and join the military. I don't care which branch, just pick one and get yourself out of this town and someplace where they'll teach you discipline and give you a sense of purpose."

As much as I didn't want to hear it at the time, I knew Grandma was right. She'd been raising me and Jared since our parents died, having moved to North Haven just so we boys could finish high school without relocating to live with her in DC. But I didn't appreciate her sacrifice. I resented everyone.

To spite her and the whole world, I picked the most dangerous career in the most dangerous branch I could think of, and I became a Marine.

At first I was on a suicide mission. Anyone who could kill their own parents deserved to die. But over time, a brotherhood formed between me and the men I served with. They became my family, and I had a reason to live.

But then I killed them too by not seeing the ambush that would ultimately take their lives.

When it came time for me to reenlist after eight years in the Marine Corps, I knew I owed it to the guys who were still left. I had to get out, so maybe they'd have a chance.

I was like a curse, and I refused to take them down with me.

I didn't tell a soul I was coming home to North Haven, not even my brothers. I knew they'd want to throw me some ridiculous welcome home party, and that was the last thing I deserved.

According to Dad's will and the division of his assets, I had inherited Cole Lodge, which was a giant cabin and wilderness resort Dad had built years before I was born. Some local environmentalist group had claimed it violated the habitat of an endangered salamander. The controversy kept Dad from officially opening the lodge, and it had been abandoned ever since. I had a crazy idea that maybe I could finish what Dad had started, and give wilderness tours out of the place.

A little cabin had been built behind the lodge for the manager to live in. It was small, but perfect for me. It was completely isolated, deep in the woods, and I knew no one would bother me out there.

Eventually, word got out that I had returned home and was living in the cabin. I made sure to let folks know I wanted to be left alone, and I wasn't afraid to get nasty if that's what it took. It made me realize maybe Dad wasn't as big an asshole as everyone thought he was. Maybe he just needed to become one so people would give him some peace.

All I wanted was to live alone in my cabin where I couldn't hurt anyone, and maybe give the occasional guided tour through the forest to schoolkids and tourists. Nothing dangerous, just some nice, easy nature walks and survival skills workshops. I had to do something good in the world, no matter how small, and this was one thing I could do.

Other than that, I'd keep to myself.

Of course, that was before I met Audrey Sawyer. I was drawn to her like a magnet, and even when I tried to drive her away, she found a way to haunt my dreams.

FIVE
AUDREY

"Welcome to the grand opening of Pine Creek Lodge," Sean Rutherford greeted me as I stepped off the big yellow school bus, with twenty-seven thirteen-year-old faces pressed against the windows.

As the students poured off the bus, Sean shook my hand gratefully and said, "I can't thank you enough for booking your field trip with us. In a town like North Haven, word-of-mouth advertising is the surest way to let everyone know we are now open for business."

"You gave the school an unbeatable deal, and after that, getting permission from the school board was a piece of cake," I assured him.

Sean had always been congenial since the first day I met him. Noah's abrasive personality had briefly made me hesitate about going through them for the field trip, but after learning about Noah's haunted past, I felt a lot more forgiving of his off-putting nature.

"You probably had a much tougher time convincing the parents to sign the permission slips," a snarky voice said over my shoulder.

I turned to see Noah Cole standing there with a backpack slung over his shoulder. I could see his pecs bulging under his fitted shirt, and it made my body tingle.

"Actually, that part wasn't as hard you might expect," I said.

"Sorry, buddy, it sounds like you're not as notorious as you like to think you are." Sean slapped him on the back, and I was surprised to see Noah stretch his long arm around Sean's shoulder in a brotherly hug and laugh.

Before that moment, I never would have guessed Noah was capable of being light-hearted, and I had to admit I liked seeing him that way. I would have liked to make the moment last longer, but the kids were beginning to roughhouse and tease each other, and I remembered that I actually had a job to do.

"We better contain the troops before they get out of hand," I said and called my students to attention. "Class, this is Mr. Cole. He'll be leading us on our hike today. I want you all to pay careful attention to what he says. You each have your bingo card with the names of some of the animal and plant species you need to identify during the hike. The first student to get bingo in any direction will win a special prize."

"Bingo?" Noah snatched one of the spare cards I was carrying from my hand and looked at it with a scowl.

"What's wrong with bingo?" I asked, a defensive edge to my voice despite my best effort to remain cool.

He ignored me.

"All right, kids," Noah called out in a clear, resonant voice that commanded attention. "The first thing I want you to do is take your bingo card, fold it up as small as you can make it, and shove it in your pocket."

"What are you doing?" I asked, horrified. I'd put a lot of

work into designing that lesson plan, and now he was asking them to destroy it.

Looking at all the kids, Noah said, "You can't focus on what's around you if you've got your mind on some bingo card. Today, I want a hundred percent of your attention on the forest, the trees, the leaves, the moss, the plants growing all around you. The birds singing on the branches and the animals hiding beneath the foliage. There is so much to see and hear and experience in the forest, if you turn your eyes away for one moment, you might miss something incredible."

The students were all nodding, already enraptured, and I had to admit Noah was good. Suddenly, he pointed into the distance and all the kids turned and gasped. So did I.

"Did you see that?" Noah asked with an air of excitement.

"Was it a deer?" one student asked.

"Was it a chipmunk?" another asked.

"No," Noah said, lowering his voice as if he had a secret to share. "It was a maple leaf falling to the forest floor. Look under your feet and you'll see more. Can you guess what animals feed off this tree?"

The students hovered around him, eager to learn the secrets of the forest. As much as I hated to admit it, I was impressed at how good Noah was at gaining their attention and keeping it. I knew from experience just how hard that could be.

Noah talked for hours, guiding the students through the forest along a clearly marked trail, but occasionally leading them off it to show them something special.

"If you look up there, you'll see the nest of a peregrine falcon. There's the female flying overhead, and over there is the male."

up to that name. Really push the boundaries on what these kids have experienced so far, and show them new horizons."

I could see from the spark in his eyes that Noah liked where I was headed, so I plunged ahead.

"I was thinking these kids are old enough to try rock climbing, kayaking, maybe even zip-lining. But I can't do it alone. I need someone with experience to help me. So, will you do it?"

Noah's eyes were bright, and I could see the ideas churning in his brain. He took a piece of paper and started scribbling them out. I leaned in close to see, so we were practically cheek to cheek. I could smell his cologne, and feel the heat coming off his body. It made my flesh tingle. I longed to turn my face towards his and kiss him, but he'd already made it clear how he felt about me. Instead, I contented myself to lean in close to him, resting my shoulder against his strong chest.

"This would be perfect for our first club outing," I said and reached out to touch his notepad. He moved his hand at the same time, and our fingertips touched. It was electric, and the sensual chemistry between us made me tremble. Then, without warning, Noah pulled away from me. He abruptly rose to his feet, nearly causing me to fall on my ass.

Noah said coldly, "Fine. Book the appointment with Sean. I'll schedule the activity at no charge since it's for a school club. If nothing else, it will make for a nice tax write-off."

"Thanks." I sat there, feeling confused and more than a little hurt. Noah was so warm and friendly with the kids and with Sean, but anytime he was alone with me, he recoiled. Why did he dislike me so much? What had I ever done to him?

Maybe he just found me physically repulsive. Maybe

Wayne Thornton was right when he said I was nothing if I wasn't with him. No, I knew Wayne was an abusive asshole, and I refused to play victim for him, but it was clear Noah didn't want anything to do with me for his own reasons.

I swallowed the lump in my throat.

I was hopelessly attracted to the one man in town who couldn't stand to be around me, and I didn't even know why.

SIX

NOAH

I woke like I always did, sitting bolt upright in bed, sweating and shaking. It took me a moment to realize the sound I heard wasn't my ears ringing from an exploded bomb, but the sound of my goddamn cell phone.

"What?" I barked into the phone, anxious to shut the fucking noise off.

"Well, good morning to you too." Sean greeted me, and suddenly I felt like a giant asshole.

"Sorry. I just woke up. What's going on?" It was rare for Sean to call me so early in the morning, but then I caught a glimpse of the clock on the wall and noticed it wasn't nearly as early as I first thought.

"I was just wondering if you'd been to the lodge yet, or turned on the morning news," Sean said, and he sounded serious.

"No. Why?" I was out of bed like a bolt, pulling on my black jeans and looking for my damn boots.

Sean breathed a frustrated sigh and said, "Well, the good news is, giving that guided field trip to the middle school worked like you said it would. The word is out that we're open for business."

"So, what's the bad news?" I asked, even though I wasn't sure I wanted to know.

"Well, just walk up to the lodge and see for yourself. It's all over the local news. I'm on my way now. Don't do a thing until I get there."

Now I was really concerned. I found one boot under my bed and finally found the other one lying on its side by the chair my brother had made for me. I pulled them on, threw on a shirt, and marched down the trail from my cabin to the lodge.

I could hear them before I could see them. It was a rally being held by the fucking animal rights group Save the Salamanders.

Fuck!

They were the same damn group that had harassed my dad decades ago. They were wrong about the salamanders' habitat then, and they were just as wrong now. Couldn't they find anything better to do with their fucking time than cause mischief and spread lies?

"What the hell is this?" I shouted angrily as I took the steps of the lodge two at a time to stand in front of the crowd. I could feel the veins on my forehead throbbing. "This is private property! Get the hell out of here!"

The crowd erupted, waving their posterboard signs in the air and chanting as loud as they could, "Save the salamanders! Save the salamanders!"

Suddenly, a reporter from a Roanoke news program was shoving a microphone in my face, and for the first time I noticed his cameraman standing at the back of the crowd, focusing his lens right at me. Shit!

"Glen Strong with Channel 2 News speaking with

Noah Cole, owner of the Cole Lodge," the spray-tanned asshole grinned at me with white veneers. "Is it true this lodge was forced to close years ago, before it even opened, for encroaching on the habitat of the endangered Shenandoah salamander?"

"Not exactly." My blood was boiling.

"I did a little digging, and the original Cole Lodge was taken to court on numerous occasions for endangering the rare salamander. What do you have to say about that?"

I worked my jaw, trying to think of a response to this asshole that wouldn't create bad publicity for the lodge. This punk was probably still in diapers when my dad built this lodge, and now he was trying to make me look bad just for a ten-second spot on the back end of the news hour. I desperately wanted to punch this moron in his plastic face, just to make the human interest piece more exciting.

Glen Strong stretched his arms to encompass the crowd and said, "With this much public interest in protecting the salamander, it looks to me like the Cole Lodge is doomed to close again, this time for good."

"That's it!" I snapped, taking a step toward him. "First of all, the name of this place is the Pine Creek Lodge, so get that part straight. Second of all, my father closed the original Cole Lodge because of bad publicity drummed up by idiots like you, not because the lodge posed any real danger to the salamander. Third and most importantly, the Shenandoah salamander can only survive at elevations much higher than the lodge. You need to climb all the way up to the top of that ridge to find the habitat of that beautiful and rare creature. So if you don't know what you're talking about, you should just keep your mouth shut!"

The little dickhead blinked at me, looking pale as shit. It took him a moment to regain his composure, and then he turned to the camera and put that fake grin back on his pretty-boy face.

Just then, Sean pulled up in his hybrid car and rushed upon the scene, followed by two police cars. They were able to clear away the protesters for being on private property, and cited them for not having a permit to assemble. It was good to see them go, but I knew they'd be back soon, standing just outside the property line with their permit and their posterboard signs.

Now I understood why my father was always so moody. I was the biggest nature advocate there was, but these ignorant activists were already driving me crazy, and it was only the first day.

After the last car drove off the property, Sean and I sunk on the steps of the lodge and both sighed heavily.

"Well, there's no way that's not airing on the evening edition of the news too. Only now they have added footage of me yelling and the cops driving away the peaceful animal lovers," I said with my head in my hands.

"Well, it could be worse," Sean said, and just then my cell phone rang, as if to prove his point.

I took one look at the caller ID and groaned. "It's the partners. Shit! I bet they want to pull out of the deal."

Sean had worked hard to team up with a travel agency in Roanoke called Shenandoah Travel. Once the deal was signed, they'd send customers our way, guaranteeing consistent income for us and a small kickback for them. It was a partnership I desperately needed if I wanted the lodge to be successful. Now, I'd probably blown it with my own hotheadedness.

"Let me talk to them!" Sean said, frantically reaching for my phone. I easily held it out of his reach.

"It's my company, I'll handle it. Besides, I'm the one who

yelled at a reporter on camera. I'm a big boy. I can clean up my own mess."

I t took a lot of talking, but I managed to convince the executives with Shenandoah Travel to still meet with us. They drove all the way up from Roanoke so they could see the lodge for themselves.

I worked my ass off for five days straight getting the place ready for them. I had the wood surfaces shining like new and the glass so clear you could walk through it if not for the specially made Pine Creek Lodge decals I'd carefully placed on all the windows and doors.

"This is a mighty fine-looking lodge you've got," Mr. Harris, the top dog, said with hesitation.

"But what?" I asked, my neck muscles tight.

"But, we had no idea when we first gained an interest in partnering with you how much deep-seated controversy that involved. Endangered animals, violent outbursts, threatening reporters. I just don't know if we can recommend your lodge to our clients if they're going to be subjected to this kind of thing."

"I understand that, Mr. Harris, but please, the newscast that morning was completely unfounded. There hasn't been another incident all week. The Pine Creek Lodge does not present any danger to the Shenandoah salamander. In fact, because it breathes through its skin, the salamander requires a much cooler climate that can only be found at higher elevations. You'd have to travel way up to the top of the ridge to be even close to their habitat."

"So why all the protesters?" Mr. Harris wanted to know.

"Quite simply, ignorance of the facts. They love animals and want to protect them. I do too. That's why I don't have any hard feelings over their misplaced passion. They probably saw that the group protested the lodge twenty years ago when it first opened, and out of an abundance of passion, thought they'd better protest it again now. But in the days since, I'm sure they've come to realize the truth, the lodge does not present any danger to the salamander, and so they've given up their crusade for a better cause that actually deserves their attention. I've got all the scientific data right here. You can see for yourself, the lodge does not endanger the salamander, and the courts agreed. All cases against my father were dismissed twenty years ago."

"All right. We'll recommend you to our clients on a probationary basis, but if there is even a whisper of controversy, we are pulling out of the deal," Mr. Harris said, and I was finally able to breathe again.

I let Sean be in charge of hashing out all the details. A contract was created, and we all signed it. It felt surprisingly good, like now the Pine Creek Lodge was a real business. I finally understood that sense of pride my father felt when he came home from work each night. It was invigorating, and I felt good for having taken an abandoned building in the woods and turning it into something real and wonderful.

I shook hands with Mr. Harris and his partners, and Sean and I watched as they drove away.

I grabbed two cold beers from the fridge and popped the tops, handing one to Sean and keeping the other for myself.

"We did it," I said, and tapped the neck of my bottle to his in a toast.

"We sure did." Sean grinned dopily.

Suddenly there was a loud crash that had me pushing Sean to the ground protectively. When nothing else happened, we got up and walked across the lodge to the front door.

Someone had thrown a rock through the window.

"Fuck!" I hissed under my breath, adrenaline still coursing through my veins.

There was a painted image of a salamander on the rock.

Thank God the partners had already left. But I had no idea how I was going to keep these fanatics from ruining my reputation or my business.

SEVEN

AUDREY

It was Saturday morning, and I couldn't get the smile off my face.

It had been a really good week at work, one of the best I'd had since becoming a teacher. The kids had loved the field trip, and it had reinvigorated their interest in learning and science. They even managed to pass the test I'd given on Friday, which made me feel like maybe I was actually succeeding at teaching them something.

Elisa, Bethany, and Lauren were coming at noon to take me out for a ladies' brunch, which allowed for me to sleep in, do some yoga, and have a lazy morning. It felt really good to have girlfriends again. I never realized just how much I'd missed things like brunch and happy hour, or just plain gossiping in the teachers' lounge during lunch.

It was startling to realize how badly Wayne had been isolating me. Now that I had escaped from him, I was finally able to make friends on my own, and they filled a need in me I didn't even know was lacking. Human beings needed socialization to thrive, and I was finally doing just that.

It was amazing how happy and free I felt here in North

Haven. All the stress and difficulty sleeping I'd suffered in Charlotte was gone. I could breathe easier and every morning I woke up feeling refreshed and ready to start the day. It was like I was a whole new version of myself, one that was braver, friendlier, laughed more, and was willing to take more chances.

I never fully appreciated all the little things in life until they were taken away from me. Wayne was clever about it, chipping away at my freedom bit by bit, so I didn't notice. First he changed the foods I ate, and the clothes I wore. Then he changed the hobbies I engaged in and the people I hung out with. I was like a frog sitting in a pot of water, slowly being boiled to death because the temperature of the stove was raised so subtly it never even realized it was in danger.

Wayne appeared warm and charming, but he was really deadly. I was just thankful I realized what he was doing to me before I became so lost I could never find myself again.

I remembered the moment I came to my senses.

It was my birthday, and he had prepared a fancy dinner. He'd claimed it was all my favorite foods, only none of them were. They were *his* favorites.

In that moment I could see what my life would be like if I became his wife, and I realized I wouldn't be me anymore. So I refused his proposal and ran outside in the rain. He didn't follow me out, or offer me his coat or an umbrella. He just left me out there, convinced that when I got cold enough, I'd come back to him.

Only I never did.

Wayne was such a far cry from Noah Cole, who looked mean but was really sweet. Seeing Noah with the kids at the lodge and how patient and kind he had been only made me even more attracted to him than I had been before.

Nearly every night, I had to stop myself from going for a jog towards his cabin, hoping to run into him.

He'd made his feelings for me, or rather his lack of feelings, crystal clear on multiple occasions now. I decided to save myself more heartache and humiliation and take the hint. Still, my dreams were filled with him at night, and I caught myself fantasizing about him during the day.

I decided to do a quick check of my emails before the girls came to pick me up for brunch. My mother had promised to send me pictures of my sister's new baby, and I needed to pay some bills too.

As I scrolled through my inbox, sending the junk to my spam folder as I went, I saw something that made my heart stop.

Hesitantly, I decided to click on it. It was an email from Wayne Thornton.

Hey, baby,

I miss you. Do you miss me?

I dropped in on your folks, and they say they haven't heard from you since we broke up. You should warn them not to put their garbage cans out the night before pickup. Anyone could go through them. They must have loved the basket you sent them of Appalachian delicacies, because all the wrappers were empty.

I've been thinking of taking a trip to Virginia lately. I hear Richmond is a good place to have a wedding, or maybe Chesapeake, or Suffolk. There are a lot of places you could be hiding, but not for long.

With a love like ours, I'm guaranteed to find you, and I won't stop till I do.

Love always, your devoted fiancé,

Wayne

A chill ran down my spine. My stomach twisted in nausea, and I ran into the bathroom to wretch.

He knew I was in Virginia. I'd thought he would give up on me, let me go. But he wasn't going to. The idea made me feel lightheaded.

I was still hiding under the covers, trembling, when the girls showed up to take me to brunch.

"What's wrong?" Elisa ran up and put her arms around me.

I told them everything about Wayne and let them read his email.

"Delete it!" Bethany cried out, but Lauren stopped her.

"No, save it for the judge. We'll get a restraining order against his ass, and if he dares to violate it, we'll kick the shit out of him!"

"Lauren, wow!" I felt touched by her passion.

"Cougars have claws!" Lauren made a clawing motion with her manicured nails, and we all laughed.

It felt good to be surrounded by friends who had my back, but I still felt unnerved.

I got dressed after that and let them take me out to brunch at a cute little place downtown famous for making the best French toast, but all we were interested in were the mimosas.

"No way is that jerk going to stop you from living your life!" Elisa insisted. "He's just fishing right now, hoping you'll respond and tell him he's on the right track. There are over sixty sizable cities in Virginia, and he obviously isn't even thinking about a small, out-of-the-way town like North Haven."

I knew she was right. I'd ordered the package of Southern Appalachian treats for my parents from an online store, so the box hadn't been postmarked at the North

Haven post office. Still, it gave Wayne a clue about the region I was hiding out in.

"And if he does show up here, we'll sic Lauren on him!" Bethany said, and Lauren made her clawing gesture again with a playful roar.

"Thanks, y'all. I needed this," I said, and suddenly my eyes filled with unbidden tears.

"Whoa, what's with the waterworks?" Elisa passed me a napkin to dab my eyes, and the three of them all got up from the table to wrap their arms around me.

"It's just been such a long time since I had friends, real friends like you. It just feels really good," I said, completely overcome with emotion.

We spent the whole day together, talking and shopping and ending with a movie. By the end of the day, I'd completely forgotten about Wayne and was back to thinking about Noah, only I didn't tell the girls about that.

I still hadn't told anyone about my feelings for Noah Cole. My friends had all warned me to stay away from him, and the rest of the town didn't seem to like him too well, especially after he'd supposedly almost beaten up some Roanoke reporter and kicked the members of an animal rights group off his property.

But I knew the real Noah, the one who could identify every leaf that grew in the forest. The quiet ex-Marine who liked chopping firewood and kept a beautifully hand-carved chair by the wood stove in his private cabin deep in the woods. The mountain man who invited a complete stranger into his home, just because he knew she was cold, and warned her to buy warmer clothes, even if he said it a bit too gruffly.

Noah Cole was a man who cared about other people, even as he wanted to isolate himself away from them. He loved nature, and the forest, and being outdoors. He loved handcrafted items, kindness, and beauty. Most of all, he loved to protect others and felt a deep sense of responsibility if he perceived that he had failed.

Noah was all heart. It was just too bad that his heart was scarred and bruised. I wished he would let me in so I could help mend it, but I knew he never would.

He was also a man who liked to be alone.

As I drifted off to sleep that night, my dreams were of Noah.

I was blissfully unaware a nightmare had just arrived in town, desperately clutching a photo of me.

EIGHT

NOAH

"Did an animal chew through it?" Sean asked, holding up the severed cord for our generator like it was a snake that might bite him.

"No, chewing would have left the ends frayed," I said, relieving him of the cord and examining it unhappily. "That's a clean cut, from a knife. This is deliberate sabotage."

"I'll file a report with the police department," Sean said, always doing things by the book. "They probably won't be able to catch the vandals, but at least it will go on record."

"Sounds good." I nodded. "When you're done, can you swing by the hardware store and pick up a new generator? I'll give you cash, since the manager's still being a dick."

"Don't you want to file a claim through our insurance and let them cover the cost?" Sean asked. He almost sounded disappointed that he wouldn't get to fill out the claim forms. Once a nerd, always a nerd.

"Nah. It'll be faster and easier just to pay for it myself, and we can't risk having our insurance canceled right now with Shenandoah Travel watching our every move. They've already given us more business in referrals than we've gotten on our own since the day we opened. We can't risk having them drop us just because some teenager was probably acting out on a dare."

"Whatever you say, you're the boss," Sean said.

"No, we're partners," I reminded him. I may have done the financial backing and the heavy lifting, but Pine Creek Lodge never would have worked as a business without his brilliant mind managing everything. I was proud to have him for my partner, and I never wanted him to forget it.

"All right, partners." Sean grinned as I hefted the generator into the back of his hybrid. The weight of it sunk the rear of his car so low to the ground, I feared he might scrape the undercarriage of his vehicle on the uneven road leading away from the lodge, but he made it out fine.

I decided to do a safety check around the perimeter of the lodge, and a supply count, just in case anything else had been damaged or stolen. I was just finishing up when Audrey Sawyer pulled up in her sleek car, with its heated seats and automatic parking features.

"What are you doing here?" I barked. I realized it made me sound like I wasn't happy to see her, when in reality I was a little too happy. Damn, she was beautiful! I turned my back on her, so she wouldn't see me have to adjust the erection that was forming in my jeans.

"I thought we should go over the itinerary for the Explorers Club outing coming up on Saturday," she said. Her long chestnut ponytail was pulled through the back of her baseball cap, and she was wearing blue jeans, a thermal shirt, hiking boots, and a puffy vest. It looked like she'd spent a fortune at REI, but at least this time she was more prepared for the outdoors.

"I've got everything planned out for Saturday. You can

go back home and watch *The Bachelor* or the Kardashians, or whatever the hell it is you do on your time off," I said, feeling like I might not be able to resist the temptation to kiss her if she stayed.

Audrey pulled a stuffed backpack from her car and dropped it at my feet. With a determined glare, she said to me, "If I'm going to be responsible for the kids in that club, I'm going to need to see firsthand exactly what you're going to teach them. Now are you going to show me or do I need to go through your competition?"

"What competition?" I glared. There was only one guy I could think of, and I prayed to God she wouldn't say his name.

"Hathaway Hunting and Fishing," Audrey said with a lift of her chin, and I felt my gut roil.

"Paul Hathaway wouldn't know an animal track from an antler up his ass. He's been charging tourists to guide them through these woods for years, but folks would be better off following a blind dog with no sense of smell than listening to his bullshit. He's the bastard that turned me in for violating the salamander habitat, but if he knew the first damn thing about them, he'd know that accusation was false. He was just trying to get me shut me down so he wouldn't have the competition. He's a total asshole!"

"So, does that mean we're on for the afternoon?" Audrey asked, with her arms crossed in front of her chest and her chocolate eyes sparkling. I was dying to wipe that smug smirk off her beautiful face.

"Fine," I acquiesced, but I made damn sure she knew I wasn't happy about it. "I thought for their first outing, the kids should learn what to do if they were ever lost in the woods. Including how to build a lean-to shelter, and how to make fire."

"I want you to show me step by step, before you teach the kids. I have a responsibility to know ahead of time everything they'll be doing."

"Sure, but the sun will be setting soon," I said. "Are you prepared to be out after dark this time, city slicker?"

"I am if you are." Audrey hefted her pack onto her shoulders with confidence, and I couldn't help but admire her spirit.

"All right then, let's go," I said, grabbing the bag I always kept at the ready.

I hiked her uphill, through dense brush, trying to wear her out, but for a schoolteacher, Audrey was in incredibly great shape. It must have been all that jogging and yoga she always did. No wonder her ass was so fine!

"So, the sun is getting low and it's obvious we won't be able to make it out of the woods before dark," I said, using the teaching tone I'd used when talking to the students. "The first thing you'll need to do is erect a shelter to protect your body from the elements, like rain, snow, and frost. Keeping warm and dry is the best way to prevent hypothermia or frostbite, which can result in loss of limb or even death."

"Less doom and gloom, and more hands-on learning," Audrey said, giving me constructive criticism that I hadn't asked for, and didn't need.

"Start trying to find some branches that are at least this long." I held up a branch for an example, resisting the urge to snap it in two out of anger. God, she could be frustrating!

Audrey worked with surprising diligence and produced a good pile of branches that nearly equaled what I was able to gather. Of course, I had given her the easier area to search, while I took the more challenging one.

"Okay, very good. Now we can erect a lean-to shelter by positioning the branches like this," I said.

Audrey snickered.

Glaring at her, I snapped, "What?"

"Nothing."

She snickered again, and I couldn't help but notice how adorably sexy her smile was when she was trying to hide it. I glared at her even harder, until she finally confessed what was so funny. "It's just that you want to avoid using words like *erect* when teaching seventh graders. I know it's juvenile, but that's what they are, and if you give them any kind of fuel for a dirty joke, that's right where their immature, hormone-infused minds will go."

"Okay, fine. You want to *build* a lean-to shelter," I said with exaggerated emphasis on the word replacing *erect*. I saw her point though, and now that the double entendre had been put into my mind, I was having a hard time not thinking about erections. It made it hard to concentrate on my work, especially being so close to Audrey. Damn, she was sexy, but I had to force myself to stay on task.

We managed to get the lean-to shelter completed just as the final rays of light were fading into darkness.

"Now what?" Audrey said. She was putting on a brave front, but I could tell from the very subtle inflections in her voice and her body language that she was growing more anxious as the sky became darker.

"Now we build a fire. Did you bring any matches?"

"No, I thought you'd have some." Audrey's eyes were huge. "Please tell me you have matches."

"Sorry." I held up my empty hands as if to prove it.

"You're kidding!" Audrey cried aloud, looking utterly ashen. Now it was my turn to stifle a laugh.

"Actually, I'm not kidding. I thought this would be a

good learning point for the kids. Always pack matches when going on a hike, even if you think you'll only be gone a few hours. Nobody ever plans to get lost in the woods, so you have to prepare for the unexpected. Let me show you how to build a fire if you're ever stranded in the woods with no matches."

"I know how," Audrey snapped.

"I'm sure you do, but please let me," I offered, but she held up her hand.

"I'm not just some helpless city girl. I can build a fire!" Audrey insisted. She gathered bits of tinder and dried leaves, fashioned two sticks and started to rub them together.

I could tell this was going to take a while, so I opened my pack and began to set up camp. I unrolled my sleeping bag, set out some space blankets, my water bottle and beef jerky, and leaned back comfortably against a log to watch the show.

"This is impossible!" Audrey cried out in frustration after only a few minutes had gone by.

"Well, it is if you're doing it like that," I said, and took the sticks from her soft hands. There was a spark of attraction between us when our fingers touched that startled us both, and yet was undeniable. Speaking softly, I said, "They may depict starting a fire like that in the movies, but there's a much better way in real life. When we teach the kids, the sun will still be out and they'll have plenty of time to practice. We can make a contest out of it, and the first student to make a fire will win a prize."

"I'd consider it a prize just to have fire right now," Audrey said, visibly shivering.

"In that case, let's speed things along," I said, and pulled my lighter out of my back pocket. I held it to the tinder and within moments, I had a small fire going. I added a few sticks, and then some bigger ones, and soon there was a cozy little fire blazing happily before us.

I thought Audrey would be grateful for the warmth, but that just showed how little I knew I about women.

"You had a lighter this whole time, and you let me make a fool of myself trying to rub those sticks together!" Audrey was enraged.

"Hey, don't blame me. You're the one who said you could do it yourself, remember?"

"That's because you lied to me! You said you didn't bring anything to start a fire with!"

"Actually, I said I didn't bring any matches. That wasn't a lie. And I did offer to build the fire. You just refused to let me, because city girls are bossy know-it-alls who can't listen to anybody."

"You arrogant, condescending ass!" Audrey cried out in a hostile rage.

Then suddenly, without warning, she flung herself at me, and before I could stop her, she had her lips on mine and was kissing me with a fiery embrace unlike anything I'd felt before.

I knew I should stop her. I knew I should push her away, but instead I pulled her into my arms and kissed her back.

NINE
AUDREY

All I could think about was how crazy Noah was driving me, how wildly irritating he was with that cocky grin of his, and how wild and crazy it made me feel just to be near him. My blood was raging, my heart was pounding, and my body was trembling. Then, the next thing I knew, I was kissing him. I had flung myself on top of him and was taking his mouth with my own.

Noah's large hands gripped me. I expected him to peel me off him and ask me what the hell I was doing, but that wasn't what happened. Instead, those strong hands wrapped around me, holding me close, as his lips parted and the kiss deepened.

My body melted under his embrace. A soft moan escaped my throat.

"Noah, I want you," I whispered as he began nibbling my ear, driving me wild with desire as we lay back onto his sleeping bag.

"Audrey, you're so fucking sexy," he murmured. "I've wanted you too, since the first moment I saw you."

It was all I needed to hear. I began stripping off my clothes, flinging them to the side and into the shrubs. Noah stripped off his clothes too, but with less to remove, he was finished a lot faster. God, his body was magnificent, rippling with bulging muscles. I saw several scars, deep and ugly, marring his perfect flesh. Moving cautiously, I gently touched them with my open palm as I ran my hand over his torso.

"Do they hurt?" I asked in a low voice.

"Not as much as memories do," Noah said. He took my breasts into his hands and fondled them seductively. With lustful eyes, he said throatily, "Right now, I just want to feel good."

Then he brought his mouth down onto my breasts. His mouth was like magic, bringing me pleasure I'd never felt before. I ran my hands against his short-cropped hair, holding him to me. As Noah's hot, wet mouth suckled the nipple of one breast, he used his forefinger and his thumb to gently roll and pinch my other nipple. Moans of pleasure tore from my throat as I arched my back, pressing my tits towards him, wanting more.

When he'd had his fill, Noah kissed his way down my stomach, to the triangle between my legs. I spread my thighs wide, welcoming him in. I expected him to dive right in, but he used his fingers first, gently massaging me there until I was soaking wet while his mouth took mine with passionate kisses.

"Are you sure you want to do this?" Noah asked, even as he slipped on a condom.

"Yes. Fuck me now, right here in the woods where we met," I panted, helping him secure the condom in place. His rigid cock flexed under my touch, and I enjoyed pleasuring him that way for a moment, running my hand up and down the length of him while he groaned with pleasure.

He entered me then, with a slow, steady pressure as I wrapped my arms and legs around him, and moaned with ecstasy.

"Oh, God. You feel so good," I cried aloud as he sunk in all the way to the hilt.

"So do you, even better than I fantasized," Noah buried his lips in my neck, kissing my throat as he began to thrust within me.

"Not too fast. Make it last," I panted, as I ran my nails down his back to clutch his round, firm ass. As I squeezed him there, Noah groaned and plunged into me even deeper, stealing my breath away, as intense ripples of pleasure pulsed through me.

I rocked my hips in rhythm with his own, driving every thrust harder and deeper within me as the waves of pleasure kept growing bigger and stronger.

"Oh, God, I'm coming!" I cried aloud, my voice echoing through the forest. I'd never felt such intense pleasure in my whole life.

My nails dug into the flesh of Noah's ass, driving him to pump faster and harder as my orgasm just kept going. I saw him bite his lower lip and contort his face in glorious ecstasy, and I knew that he was climaxing along with me.

Afterwards, he wrapped a blanket around my shoulders, and we cuddled in front of the fire. I couldn't remember the last time I'd felt so relaxed and happy. Certainly, sex with Wayne had never been like this.

"I'm sorry about the matches," Noah said with chagrin as he stroked my hair tenderly.

"That's okay. I may have been acting a bit stubborn

about building the fire, but you did a great job. Too bad we don't have ingredients for s'mores. If we did, then tonight would be perfect."

"Well, actually..." Noah reached into his bag and pulled out graham crackers, marshmallows, and a Hershey bar. Grinning cockily, he said, "Always be prepared when you go into the woods."

He found two sticks, used his pocketknife to sharpen them to a point, and handed one to me.

"You must have been quite the Boy Scout," I said as I skewered a marshmallow with my stick and held it over the fire.

"Not quite. I was a real troublemaker when I was a kid. With three older brothers, and an adorable baby behind me, I had to work hard to gain my father's attention, and I wasn't afraid to use whatever means necessary. Not that it ever worked. Dad only had eyes for business."

"What about your mother?" I asked him, feeling empathetic.

"She was the complete opposite of Dad. Warm, loving, doting. I'd been a difficulty pregnancy and nearly died of complications shortly after birth, so she had a special place in her heart for me. She called me her miracle baby, and pretty much gave me anything I wanted if I just made this face."

Noah pouted out his lower lip and turned his eyes upward in the most adorable puppy-dog face I'd ever seen.

"Aww! Here, this is for you!" I laughed, giving him my marshmallow, which I'd carefully toasted to a perfect golden brown.

"See, it works every time!" Noah laughed, and he gave me his marshmallow to make up for it.

We spent the evening talking and laughing under the

star-filled sky, sharing stories of our childhoods, our hopes and dreams, and even a few secrets. Afterwards, we made love again until we drifted off to sleep, cuddled together in Noah's sleeping bag, next to the warm glow of the embers of the campfire.

TEN

NOAH

"Okay, so I'll see you on Saturday with the Explorers," I said, feeling awkward as I loaded Audrey's pack into the trunk of her car.

"It's a date." Audrey's smile was dazzling, and all I wanted to do was make love to her again.

"Okay. Drive safe." I leaned on the driver's side door and kissed her goodbye, not wanting to let her go.

"I'm going to be late for class and I still have to go home, shower and change," Audrey said, gently forcing me to back away as she slowly drove forward. "What would my students think if they saw me like this?"

"You look beautiful!" I insisted.

"Yeah, right!" Audrey laughed in jest, then she plucked a leaf from her messy hair and threw it out the car window at me as she drove away.

I watched until her car completely disappeared from my sight, and then walked slowly back towards the lodge with a dopey grin on my face.

Last night had been incredible. Making love to Audrey had been even more amazing than I'd dreamed it would be.

She had such a spark that she brought to everything she did, from teaching to fucking, and I admired her so much for her strength of spirit and unwavering passion.

We woke with the sunrise, snuggled together by the ashes of the fire, and marched double-time back through the forest. The pace was so brisk, we didn't talk much, but Audrey was determined to get to work on time, and I knew better than to argue with her about it.

I would have liked to have made her breakfast, and spent the morning talking about what last night meant. Were we going to date now? Was it going to happen again?

The thought made my heart swell in my chest. I was grinning so wide, my fucking face hurt, but slowly that feeling morphed into one of worry and fear.

What the hell was I thinking? I couldn't let Audrey become my girlfriend. Was I completely forgetting the curse?

My mom had always praised me for living through near-death experiences that others didn't, but that miracle came with a price. A life for a life. Every time I was spared, the fates demanded blood in the form of someone I cared about. First it was my parents, then the guys in my platoon. If I let Audrey get too close, then she would undoubtedly be next.

It wasn't fair. I'd tried so hard to keep my distance from Audrey, and not to let her into my heart, but she'd found a way to slip inside my defenses. I was truly beginning to care deeply for her. Now was the time to sever that connection, and cut off any hints of romance at their root.

Just then my cell chimed. It was Audrey, letting me know she'd gotten home safely. I wanted to respond, but instead I marked the text as having been read, and then didn't reply back. No text, no emoji, not even a like. I would go completely silent, not responding to any of her calls, texts, or emails from this moment forward.

As painful as it would be, I would have to keep my distance. It would hurt her less if I didn't lead her on.

On Saturday, I would be cold and aloof. I'd uphold my obligation to teach the kids, but that was it. I wouldn't give Audrey any attention, or even look at her or talk to her beyond what was necessary. Eventually she'd ask me what was going on, and I'd tell her it was nothing more than a one-night stand. She'd be upset, but I could deal with that. It was better for her to hate my guts than to love her and let her fall victim to my curse. I'd been through enough grief and heartache. I refused to put myself through any more. It just sucked that I'd finally found someone I wanted to spend all my days and nights with, and now I had to shove her away. It was my own damn fault for spending the night with her. The blame and the guilt I felt for my own weakness filled me with anger.

I could use my anger to fortify a wall around my heart, blocking out any feelings of affection I might have had for Audrey, and making my heart as cold and hard as stone.

There was a dead tree standing near the lodge that needed to be cut down. Grabbing my ax, I swung it against the thick trunk with a vengeance, pouring out all my frustration, anger, guilt, disappointment, and heartache with every chop. I knew a chainsaw would have been faster, but something inside me needed to swing that ax.

Sweat was pouring down my back and my muscles ached when the tree was finally felled, but I wasn't done. I kept going. First, I broke off the branches by stomping them with my heavy boots until the trunk was stripped. I finally grabbed the chainsaw and attacked the trunk itself, cutting it into thick logs.

My mother's last words to me rang through my mind. She'd ruffled my hair and said, "Be good, and I'll see you tonight."

But I wasn't good that night. I'd been acting like an ass. I'd been playing pranks on my brothers while my mother was going out of her way to pick me up a treat I completely didn't deserve.

Now I was getting what I deserved. A life without love. A future living in isolation, utterly alone.

Sweat from my forehead was blinding my eyes as I took up my ax once more, this time to split the logs, turning it into firewood that could be used to heat the lodge through the winter. I was decimating what had once been tall and beautiful and turning it into nothing but a pile of logs. My breathing was labored. My arms, shoulders, and back were absolutely burning, and my hands could barely hold onto the wooden handle of the ax anymore.

It was time for me to call it quits. Reluctantly, I let the ax fall from my grip onto the forest floor and sunk down to sit on the remaining stump of the once great tree.

"Finally. I was beginning to wonder just how long you'd keep going," a voice said, and I was startled to see Sean standing there. He handed me a bottle of water and I gulped it down gratefully.

"How long have you been standing there?" I asked him, my voice a low growl. Although I knew I was out chopping wood in plain sight in the middle of the day, somehow I felt like I'd been spied on in some intimate moment and I didn't like it.

"Not long, but from the sight of that pile of wood, I'm guessing you've been punishing yourself for hours. What happened?"

"Nothing," I said unconvincingly.

"Yeah, clearly," Sean said sarcastically. I guess he figured I was too exhausted to kick his ass, and lucky for him, he was right.

I don't know how he did it, but somehow Sean got me to open up about Audrey. I confessed to him everything that happened the night before, and why I couldn't let myself fall for her. I wasn't usually into being so touchy-feely, but Sean was just so quiet and unassuming. All he had to do was sit there silently, and somehow I just told him everything, whether I wanted to or not. Like he had some nerdy superpower.

"I already know what you're going to say, so don't bother," I growled, pointing an angry finger toward his scrawny chest. "You're going to tell me none of it is my fault, not my parents' death, or the guys in my platoon, none of it. I've heard it all a thousand times from every shrink out there. I've heard it from my brothers, and even from the waitress down at the coffee shop. Everybody thinks they're a fucking psychiatrist these days, but none of them have actually seen the shit that I've seen or been through the shit that I've been through. So don't fucking pretend to know how I feel or tell me everything's going to fucking be all right."

It was an angry rant, and when I finally stopped to catch my breath, I couldn't even look Sean in the face out of fear he'd see all the pain in my eyes.

"I wasn't going to," Sean said quietly, with his damn superpower again. But I refused to give into it quite so easily.

"Damn straight!" I said emphatically. "You were raised by both your mom and your dad when I was living with my grandmother, and you were safe and sound stateside while I was taking shrapnel in Afghanistan, watching my entire platoon get wiped out in a fucking ambush. So if I tell you I don't want to be in a relationship ever in my whole life, then you'd better not say a goddamn word about it!"

"You're absolutely right," Sean agreed again, stealing what was left of the wind from my sails. I was angry and ready to pit all my energy against anyone with the guts to debate me, but Sean's passive acquiescence gave me nothing to rail against, and I was left utterly defeated. "I wasn't there, man," Sean said. "I haven't been through any of the tragic things you've seen. In fact, my life's been pretty golden, thanks to you. Remember when TJ was going to shove me into the dumpster behind the cafeteria, and then you showed up?"

"Yeah, he pissed his pants and went running." I chuckled fondly at the memory.

"I don't know if I ever thanked you for that day," Sean said.

"Sure you did. You thanked me like ten times in a row before the bell even rang."

"No, not for scaring TJ, for the way that day changed my whole life."

"What the fuck are you talking about?" I thought the geeky little guy had finally lost it.

"That day you stopped TJ from throwing me into the dumpster was the day I met Jenna," Sean said with a flush.

"Your wife? No shit!" I mused with a chuckle. They were the perfect couple, two nerds in love, and I was truly happy for him and how good their marriage was.

"After you went chasing after TJ and I was alone, Jenna came out of the cafeteria. She asked me if I was all right, and invited me in to clean my scrapes. Her touch was so gentle, I fell in love with her right then. You ever have that feeling? Ah, of course you have. I've seen the way you look at Audrey. But Jenna and I probably never would have met if it weren't for you, and I don't think I ever thanked you for that day. It was the moment that changed my whole life for the better. When I heard you'd signed up for the Marine Corps, it gave me the courage to ask her on our first date. The day I graduated college, I asked her to marry me. And today, she told me we're expecting our first child."

It took a moment for the words to sink in, but when they did, my eyes flew open wide and I grabbed Sean hard and hugged him. "Jenna's pregnant? You two are having a baby! Congratulations, buddy! That's so fucking great. I couldn't be happier for you."

"Thanks." Sean had to blink back tears of joy, or maybe I'd accidentally bruised a rib by hugging him too hard. In either case, he was beaming with pride. He shook my hand and said earnestly, "You deserve this kind of happiness, too."

"Shut up," I said, my voice low like an animal warning away an intruder.

"I'm serious," Sean insisted. "You deserve love and happiness as much as anybody, certainly as much as me. What have I ever done in life? I'm just a geeky nerd who couldn't stand up to a high school bully. You did that for me. Then you went off to war and bravely protected our country. You think the things you've seen and the sacrifices you've suffered mean you don't deserve love, but I'm telling you, buddy, I think the opposite is true. I think they mean you deserve love more. You just have to open your heart and let it in, instead of walling yourself off and keeping love out."

"You don't know a fucking thing about what I deserve," I growled.

"I know it's scary to open yourself up to heartbreak, especially after all you've lost, but the joys are worth the risk. I've seen the way Audrey brings out the best in you. She's strong and independent. She's your perfect match. Don't push her away out of fear. You'll be missing out on the best things life has to offer, and you deserve to experience the joys and not just the pain. Take the risk."

"Don't tell me what to do. You don't know the first fucking thing about pain," I said angrily, then I turned my back on him, and walked away.

"Good morning," I sang as I waltzed into the teachers' lounge with a box of donuts. "I didn't have time for breakfast before work today, so I thought I might as well pick up enough for everyone."

"What's got you feeling so perky this morning?" Elisa eyed me suspiciously, but when I set the box of donuts down on the table in front of her and opened the lid, her attention was immediately diverted. "Oh, chocolate sprinkles!"

"I guess I just slept really well last night, and I'm glad tomorrow is Saturday. I've got my first Explorers outing and I'll get to spend the whole day out at Pine Creek Lodge."

"Oh, yeah, I forgot all about that. How's that going?" Bethany asked as she timidly selected a glazed donut from the box.

"Really good," I said, thinking of Noah and the incredible time we had last night. It wasn't just the sex, although he'd given me the best orgasm I'd ever had in my entire life. It was the way we'd really connected last night. Noah had opened up to me about his life in ways I never would have expected. His exterior was so tough, who would have guessed he was so sensitive on the inside? When he talked about his mother, the look on his face melted my heart, and when he talked about his brothers, I laughed so hard, my stomach hurt. Or maybe that was all the s'mores we'd eaten.

"Earth to Audrey," Elisa suddenly pulled me from my thoughts, and I was startled to realize I'd been daydreaming. "That's the bell. Care to teach your class today?"

"Yes, of course," I fumbled for my things, as Elisa scrutinized me again, twirling one red lock of hair around her finger, and then letting it loose to spring back into a tight curl. "Something's up with you today. I can't quite figure out exactly what it is, but something is definitely going on."

"*I* know," Lauren whispered playfully as she passed by us both on the way to her class. "She finally got laid last night."

Bethany laughed at the outrageousness of Lauren's joke as she followed the rest of the faculty as they exited the teachers' lounge, ready to start the first class period of the day. Only Elisa focused on my flushing cheeks and darting eyes to realize Lauren had accidentally guessed the truth.

"Gotta go teach. I'll talk to you later," I said quickly, and rushed past Elisa to the safety of my classroom.

"You sure will! I want details!" I heard her shout after me as I slammed my classroom door shut, and twenty-seven pairs of eyes looked up at me in surprise.

I tried to force myself to focus my attention on my students throughout the workday, but my mind kept drifting to thoughts of Noah. The touch of his lips on my body, the feel of his manhood deep inside, the way he held me close until I fell asleep. I'd texted him twice since leaving him that morning. Once to let him know I'd gotten home safely, and the second time to tell him I was at work and couldn't receive texts. I was disappointed he hadn't tried texting me back, but I guess the fact that he hadn't wasn't necessarily a bad thing, especially since I'd told him not to.

I ate lunch in my classroom in order to avoid Elisa, who would no doubt want to interrogate me about whether I'd "gotten laid." I knew I had no reason to feel ashamed. Noah and I were both single, consenting adults, and I had the right to have sex with him if I wanted to. But everybody in town had such a bias against the Cole brothers for absolutely no valid reason, especially Noah. I didn't feel like putting our relationship up to such scrutiny when it was still so new. I wanted to keep Noah and his tender sweet side all to myself for just a little while longer. After I'd had a chance to talk to Noah about it and determine where things really stood between us, then I could share the news with my girlfriends. Until then, it was really none of their business.

"Okay kids. Remember, the Explorers Club meets tomorrow morning at 8:00 sharp at the Pine Creek Lodge. Wear warm clothes and good hiking shoes, and bring your own water bottle."

"See you then, Miss Sawyer."

"Bye, Miss Sawyer. I can't wait for the hike!"

The kids all sounded happy and excited as they streamed from my classroom. It was the end of the day, and I couldn't wait for the weekend too, so I could see Noah again.

"All right, confess! Who is he?" Elisa scared the crap out of me as she burst into my classroom, looking determined to learn the truth.

"I don't know what you're talking about," I lied, but my bright pink cheeks betrayed me.

"Just tell me who he is," Elisa begged. "Lauren and

Bethany don't suspect a thing, and I promise not to say a word to them until you do first."

"Yeah, right!" I scoffed.

I grabbed my things and started to push past her through the door, when I suddenly froze.

My hands were shaking so badly I dropped everything I was holding, and it all fell to the floor with a clatter.

"What's wrong with you?" Elisa said, sounding both startled and annoyed. Then she looked at me, and her tone instantly changed.

I had pressed myself against the wall, hiding so I couldn't be seen through the doorway. All the color had drained from my flesh and my entire body was trembling.

"What's wrong? Tell me," Elisa insisted.

Jerking my head towards the hallway, I whispered, "It's him."

"The guy you did it with?" Elisa gaped, but I shook my head emphatically.

"No! It's Wayne. He just walked into the admin office. He's found me!"

"Are you sure it was him?" Elisa's green eyes were huge, and she gripped my hand and gave it a reassuring squeeze.

"I'm positive. He's going to insist I marry him, and when I refuse, he'll kill me. He's crazy!"

"Wait right here!" Elisa whispered low to me. Then she strode out my classroom door.

"Excuse me, only staff and students are allowed on school premises. You'll need to leave," I heard Elisa say forcefully.

"I'm looking for a member of the faculty. A teacher named Audrey Sawyer."

I recognized Wayne's voice instantly. It was him,

without a doubt! A chill ran down my spine, and I instinctively held my breath.

"There's no one here by that name. Sorry, you'll have to leave now or I'll have to call the police," Elisa said with conviction.

"She might have changed her name. This is her picture. Please, just tell me if you recognize her."

"Nope, never seen her before," Elisa lied. I just hoped Wayne believed her. "Why are you looking for her? Are you a private detective or something?"

"No, she's my wife, and she suffers from bouts of dementia where she forgets who she is. I just want to bring her home where I can take care of her."

"Sorry I can't help, but she doesn't live around here," Elisa said.

"All right. Well, I guess I'll be on to the next town then," Wayne said, sounding unconvinced. I heard his heavy gait as he walked out of the school and I peeked carefully through the window shades, watching as he drove away. Moments later, Elisa rushed back into the classroom.

"He's gone," Elisa assured me.

"For now, but he'll be back," I said, feeling frantic. "He knows I'm here, I could tell from his tone. I've got to get out of here! I've got to leave town right away!"

"No, you don't. Just calm down a moment." Elisa tried to soothe me. "North Haven is a small town, but you're one of us now, and we take care of our own. We'll hide and protect you. You can stay at my place tonight."

"No. I don't want to put my friends in danger. You don't know Wayne like I do. You don't know what he's capable of."

I cleaned out my desk without even looking, just blindly shoving personal items into my purse until it was bursting at the seams. When I stopped to look at Elisa, she had tears brimming in her eyes.

"You're really leaving?" Elisa cried.

"I have to. It's the only way to protect the people I care about, including you."

"This is crazy, Audrey," she pleaded. "Just slow down and let's think about it before you make any rash decisions."

I took a deep breath and shook my head. "I've already thought about it. This is what I planned to do if he found me. I have to leave now. I'm sorry."

We hugged each other tight.

"Well, let me know where you end up, so I know you're safe." Elisa gave me one last extra-big squeeze. Then she reached into her purse, pulled out a card and handed it to me.

"It's one of those pay-as-you-go debit cards. I keep it for emergencies. It's got just over a thousand dollars on it. It won't get you far, but it should help."

"I can't accept this." I thrust it back at her, but Elisa refused to take it.

"If you don't, then I won't let you leave."

"This is emotional blackmail, you know." I smiled at my best friend.

"I know. Now hurry up and get out of here. I'm going to call a buddy of mine down at the police station and see if they'll give our guest Wayne an extra hard time. If he's busy getting his car searched for a traffic violation, then you'll know you're safe to get out of town."

"Thanks, Elisa." I gave her a final hug goodbye and rushed out the door. I felt paranoid driving home, and nearly got in an accident twice looking in my rearview mirror to make sure I wasn't being followed, instead of watching the road ahead.

At my cottage, I was relieved to see my security system was intact and nobody had been on the premises. My heart was pounding as I pulled a bag from my closet and started shoving clothes into it as fast as I could. I felt heartbroken as I gave one final look around my perfect little gingerbread cottage. It had become my home, and I hated to leave it, but what choice did I have?

As I shoved my suitcase into the trunk of my car, I realized there was one final thing I had to do before I could leave town. I had to say goodbye to Noah.

TWELVE
NOAH

The practice climbing wall I'd built on the side of the lodge just needed one last thing, someone to climb it. I latched the safety rope onto my harness, and started up. The hand and footholds had been color coded, green for beginners, blue for intermediates, and red for experts. I felt confident the degree of difficulty was properly arranged, but of course, nothing beat the thrill of climbing a real cliff face with no painted stones to mark your path. There was a certain rush that came from reaching the top of a mountain with nothing to aid you but endurance, strength, and skill. It was something I would have loved to do with Audrey, if only I weren't keeping my distance from her. She'd texted me several times that morning, and twice more that afternoon, but I'd ignored them all. Sooner or later she'd get the hint. I just hoped it was sooner, before I lost my resolve and called her to tell her how much I missed her. I kept thinking about Sean's words and wondering if maybe it really was worth the risk.

As if summoned by my thoughts, Audrey's car came

speeding towards the lodge, barely screeching to a stop before crashing into the front steps.

"Hey! Are you crazy?" I shouted out, half pissed off and half scared to death that she could have really gotten hurt driving so recklessly.

I pushed off from the climbing wall and used my safety rope to slide down to the ground as she exited her vehicle, looking frantic. Seeing her like that put me in an alert state, ready for whatever was about to happen.

"I'm sorry. I just need to leave town right away, but I didn't want to go without telling you goodbye," Audrey said in a rush of words. Her hands were trembling and I'd never seen her looking so pale.

"What are you talking about?" I demanded to know.

"My ex-boyfriend, Wayne, he's here. He's found me."

"He's here?" I looked around, half expecting to see him running out of the woods towards us. She'd told me about him last night, and I wasn't a fan.

"No, not here. In North Haven. He's looking for me in town, at the school, trying to find out where I work. It won't take long before someone tells him where I live. I have to leave town before that happens."

"What happened? Did he hurt you?" I was ready to kill him if he had, but Audrey shook her head.

"No, but he said the next time he asks me to marry him, I'd better accept his proposal or he'll kill me, and I believe him. You should have seen the look in his eyes. He's crazy."

"Well, let him try and come for you here. I'll kick his ass so hard, he won't know what the fuck happened. Nobody is ever going to hurt you as long as I'm around." My blood was boiling and I wished the asshole was here in front of me so I could teach him not to threaten women.

"Thanks, but I just came to say goodbye. I don't want to put the people I care about in any danger. It's best if I just leave."

My heart dropped like a stone into my gut, and all the bullshit I'd been telling myself about how I was better off alone than with Audrey went right out the window. I couldn't resist her, and I didn't want her to go. I cared about her too much. I'd do whatever was necessary to convince her to stay.

So, I did the only thing I could think of. I pulled Audrey into my arms and kissed her, with all the passion and emotion I felt deep in my heart. She resisted for only a moment before giving in and returning the embrace. Her arms curled around my neck, pressing her tits against my chest, and making me yearn for her. I clung to her, holding her to me as tight as I could, never wanting to let her go.

"Don't go," I whispered, when we finally broke for air.

"But I have to. It's the only way—" Audrey started to say, but I cut her off.

"It's not the only way. It's just the only way that came to mind when your flight-or-fight response kicked in. It's a natural instinct, but you can overcome it with logic and make a better a choice for yourself and the ones you care about."

"What do you mean?" Audrey's big brown eyes blinked back tears, and I could see she was looking for an excuse to stay, but she was still scared.

"Stay here, in my cabin with me. Don't let that asshole run you out of the town you call home. Don't let him chase you off from your job and your friends." I hesitated for a moment, then said softly, "And from me. We'd all miss you too much. I'd miss you too much."

"But he probably already knows where I live. He's probably there now waiting for me," Audrey said, and I could see her pulse racing in her neck.

"So, don't go back there until we're sure he's left town. Stay here with me. Let me protect you."

With my arms still wrapped around her, I could feel Audrey's heartbeat starting to slow and her breathing starting to return to normal. She looked up at me with a face full of hope and said, "You'd really do that for me?"

"Of course I would. There's plenty of room in the cabin for two. You can stay as long as you want, and I have expert training in defense. If Wayne comes within a hundred feet of you, he'll regret it."

"I know how much you value your solitude. Why would you do this for me?" Audrey asked.

"Because I don't want to lose you."

She locked her eyes on mine, searching for something, then I leaned in toward her.

My mouth took hers passionately, and I pulled her soft body to mine.

We pulled apart only long enough to go to my cabin together. The moment the door closed behind us, Audrey started tearing off her clothes. She wanted me as badly as I wanted her.

God, her body was even more beautiful in the light of day, and I instantly became hard.

"Let me show you how grateful I am," Audrey cooed, and she took my dick in her hands and gently made love to me there with her hot, wet mouth.

"Fuck, you're getting me too hot," I groaned, as she took the full length of me all the way down her throat. We moved to the bed, and she stretched out across it, fully naked.

"Now it's my turn," I said, and began kissing all over the entire length of her body while she moaned and squirmed with pleasure beneath my touch. My mouth found her clit, and I sensuously ran my tongue against her most sensitive fold.

"Oh, yes," Audrey gasped, and I made love to her with my mouth, licking and lapping until she climaxed noisily beneath me. She clutched at the sheets and cried aloud, "Fuck me now. I want you inside me."

My hard dick was throbbing with desire, and I plunged inside her, sinking all the way to the hilt with one solid thrust.

"Harder. Fuck me harder," Audrey panted, and I thrust quickly, with long, powerful strokes.

"Oh, God. I'm coming again!" Audrey moaned aloud, and her cries echoed off the ceiling of my cabin as she orgasmed for the second time. I could feel her muscles spasm as I kept plunging into her tight, wet slit with wild abandon, lost in my own pleasure as I climaxed along with her. It was the most glorious, incredibly satisfying experience of my entire life, and I wondered how it was possible to feel such intense pleasure.

Afterwards, we just lay there, cuddled together side by side, too exhausted and happy to move.

"So, you'll stay then?" I asked with a grin.

"I'll stay." Audrey smiled. "I feel safe with you."

I held her until she fell asleep in my arms, but I lay awake for hours, my mind spinning like a helicopter blade.

I kept wondering if I'd made a mistake promising Audrey I could protect her. I knew I had the skills, but the possibilities for things that could go wrong were infinite. Still, I had to try, and I was determined not to fail. Seeing her looking so fearful, and hearing her say she was leaving, made me realize just how much Audrey meant to me.

I had to protect her, no matter the cost. I'd failed my parents, and I'd failed my platoon.

I would do anything to keep Audrey safe, even if it cost my own life.

"Good morning," Noah woke me with a kiss and a smile. "Did you sleep okay last night?"

Stretching my neck and shoulders, I nodded happily and said, "Better than I've slept in years. How about you? I didn't hog all the blankets, did I?"

"You did, but I didn't mind," Noah teased. I tossed my pillow at him in mock anger. He caught it easily with one hand and threw it back at me. I caught it, tucked it under me, and lay back down on it with a comfortable sigh.

"Come back to bed. It's Saturday," I said with a seductive purr.

"Aren't you forgetting a little something?" Noah arched his left brow at me, and suddenly I sat bolt upright in bed.

"The Explorers Club!"

"The Explorers Club," Noah nodded smugly.

"Where are my clothes? Where are my boots? I can't let the kids see me like this! I need some coffee! How do you find anything in this place?"

"Calm down. They won't be here for a whole hour, and if anyone arrives at the lodge early, Sean will take care of them. Why don't you start with this, and I'll find your clothes." Chuckling softly, Noah handed me a cup of steaming hot coffee. I sipped it gratefully, and felt my sanity coming back to me.

"Thank you. I needed that," I sighed, practically hugging the coffee mug.

"No problem. I've heard city girls are usually pretty worthless until they've had their coffee, but there's no fancy mochaccino latte shop around here, so you'll just have to make do with regular brew," Noah teased.

"Oh, really? What about mountain men? I heard they just eat coffee grounds straight out of the can before they trudge into the wilderness, forging new trails with nothing but a pocketknife and their bare hands."

"Not always." Noah climbed onto the bed with a playful leer. "Sometimes we just need to make love to a beautiful woman to give us the strength to forge through the wilderness."

"I see," I giggled, as I started stripping off his clothes. After all, we did have a whole hour before the kids arrived.

We made it to the lodge with ten minutes to spare, and Sean looked greatly relieved that he wouldn't have to take the Explorers hiking all on his own.

"I'm here! Sorry I'm late! I had to find more sunscreen." Just then, a very frantic-looking Elisa stumbled out of the lodge wearing hiking gear and a huge floppy sun hat, carrying two bottles of sunscreen lotion. "With my complexion, I'd be burnt to a crisp in under an hour without it."

"Well, it's a good thing the lodge had extra," I said, making Elisa look up with a scream.

"Audrey! What are you doing here?" Elisa dropped the bottles and flung herself at me, hugging me tight.

"I decided not to leave town after all," I said, feeling bad that I'd forgotten to text her last night. "Sorry about the drama yesterday. I guess I got a little carried away. But... what are you doing here?"

"Well, I knew someone had to take over the Explorers Club if you were gone, but now that you're still here, I can just sit back and relax."

"Oh, no, you don't! Noah and I could definitely use the help," I insisted.

"So it's Noah now, and not Mr. Cole, is it?" Elisa eyed me carefully.

"Yes," I said, fidgeting. "Noah said I could stay here until it was safe for me to return home, so I decided to accept his generous offer."

"Oh, really?" Elisa said, looking at me and then Noah, scrutinizing our body language as we tried to act casual and failed miserably.

With sparkling eyes and a huge grin, Elisa swatted at me and said, "So he's the one? You slept with Noah Cole! I can't believe it! Why didn't you tell me it was him?"

"I don't know. I didn't think you'd approve." I flushed, looking over as a few kids walked out of the lodge to make sure they weren't privy to this very personal information. Fortunately, they were deeply engrossed in their own conversations, and not the least bit interested in what their boring old teachers were discussing.

"Well, in that case, maybe I will chaperone, just to make sure you two are behaving yourselves on this hike."

Elisa was right. Noah and I were like a couple of kids,

exchanging secretive glances every time we thought no one was looking. It made me flirty and carefree, and I couldn't remember the last time I'd been so happy.

"I have to say, he's quite the catch," Elisa said as we walked away from the group. We relished the chance for a little girl talk while Noah worked with the kids, teaching them how to build a fire.

"I think so," I smirked playfully, and told her how our romance had bloomed over our late-night hiking trip.

"Is he always so brooding?" Elisa asked thoughtfully.

"That's just the mask he wears to keep people away. Inside he's a big teddy bear, tender and sweet. Look how patiently he works with the kids."

"Yeah, he's patient even with Tyler, who keeps mocking everything Noah says. Do they have some weird grudge against each other?"

I laughed it off, but as the day continued, I realized Elisa was right. Tyler occasionally made fun of Noah, but the other kids didn't pay him much mind. Noah regarded the boy with suspicion, and although he was always nice and polite, I got the distinct feeling Noah didn't trust him.

"Hey, everything all right?" I came up behind Noah, keeping a professional distance as I stood near him.

"It is now," Noah turned around so we were face to face, so he could gaze into my eyes flirtatiously. But then he glanced at Tyler, who was at the far side of the group. The other kids were working on a project as Sean supervised. Noah seemed immediately on edge again.

"What's going on with you?" I asked, feeling slightly concerned, but even more curious. "Are you afraid of that kid?" I joked.

"I just didn't realize he'd be part of the group."

"Why shouldn't he be?" I asked.

"Don't you know who he is?" Noah asked.

"His name is Tyler Hathaway. He's in my seventh grade biology class," I stated, not getting what the big deal could possibly be.

Noah looked at me pointedly, waiting for me to get it. When it was clear I never would, he said, "Hathaway. As in Hathaway Hunting and Fishing, my biggest rival. I've been at odds with Paul Hathaway since I decided to open this lodge. He's always trying to get me shut down, so I was just a little surprised to see his son at my lodge as a guest. Don't you think that's a little odd?"

"Tyler is a perfectly good kid. He probably joined the Explorers because he likes the wilderness just like his dad. It doesn't mean he's up to anything suspicious. He's just a kid. Give him a break."

"Maybe you're right," Noah said. "It's just hard to stop a lifetime of not trusting people. I promise to work on it."

"Good. You can start right now, with Tyler Hathaway. He came here today because you invited the Explorers Club to receive some wilderness survival training, not so you could pass judgment on who their fathers are. Do you want people to base their opinions of you on who your father was?"

"All right, you've made your point," Noah said with chagrin.

Suddenly, one of the kids shouted out excitedly, "Miss Sawyer! Mr. Cole! I did it! Fire! I made fire!"

It was one of my best students, a girl named Gabriela Montoya.

"Great job, Gabby!" her friends praised as Noah and I rushed over to see the tiny flames grow into larger ones as she carefully added small sticks to the fire.

"Congratulations, Gabby." Noah gave her a high-five.

"For winning the fire-making contest, you get a free rock-climbing lesson for you and your family. I'll give you the certificate when we get back to the lodge."

"Thank you, Mr. Cole! I've always wanted to try rock climbing." Gabby's smile was brighter than the sun.

"Me, too! Can we learn that next?"

"Can we climb up to the top of the ridge?"

The kids were all shouting at once. Everyone except Tyler. I suddenly realized he wasn't with the rest of the group anymore. I wondered if maybe Noah hadn't been right to keep an extra eye on him.

"No one can climb to the top of the ridge," said a voice.

It was Tyler. He suddenly stepped out from behind a tree and stood facing the group. Pointing up at the top of the ridge, he said knowingly, "That's the elevation where the habitat begins for the Shenandoah salamander. Violating their territory is punishable by a heavy fine. Isn't that right, Mr. Cole?"

The look the young man shared with Noah only lasted for a fraction of a second, but I saw it. Maybe Noah wasn't paranoid.

"That's right. Thanks, Tyler," Noah said with a casual grin for the sake of the group.

"Rock climbing is a bit advanced for now, but maybe in the near future, I can take you kids on the practice wall. For now, let's review the survival skills you learned today."

I watched as Noah expertly turned the kids' attention back to lean-to shelters and fire-building skills. Then he stared at them sternly and said, "Now there's only one vital skill left: how to find your way back. Does anyone know how to find your way out of the forest if you're lost?"

"Go downhill! Look for a river and follow it!"

"Find higher ground so you can get the lay of the land!" The kids all shouted out at once.

"All very good answers, and all correct," Noah said, and I couldn't help but beam with pride. In some ways, he was an even better teacher than I was, with natural charisma and a way with children. I had to work twice as hard as he did to get that level of student participation.

We let Elisa and Sean take the lead guiding the kids along the trail on the hike back to the lodge, and Noah and I lagged behind so we could pass flirty looks back and forth between each other.

"That was a really good lesson today," I praised.

"Thanks. I learned from watching my favorite teacher," Noah winked, and I felt myself blush.

We finally arrived at the lodge as the sun was starting to get low in the orange and purple sky. The kitchen staff had set out food and drinks for the starving students, and we all stuffed our faces and talked animatedly about the day.

But everyone grew silent when a black pick-up truck pulled up to the lodge and a man got out looking extremely unhappy.

"Dad! What are you doing here?" Tyler looked just like his father, only much younger.

"I should ask you the same thing." Paul Hathaway glared at his son. "Get in the damn truck right now."

"I'm here with the Explorers and Miss Sawyer. You said I could join the club," Tyler stammered as his father opened the truck door and glared for him to get in.

"I didn't realize that meant fraternizing with this scum. Hathaways believe in protecting nature so everyone can enjoy it. Not polluting the environment and killing off endangered animals. Come, on son, we're leaving right now."

Reluctantly, Tyler got in the truck. The look on his face broke my heart. I ran over to talk to Paul, hoping I could smooth things over and Tyler could still be a part of the club.

"I'll think about it," Paul responded after I'd breathlessly pleaded my case. I decided that was the best I could get for now, and watched sadly as they drove away.

Looking at Noah, I said, "Well, I guess that proves Tyler didn't come here as some kind of evil plot by his father."

"Yeah, I guess so," Noah said, but I could tell from the far-off look in his eyes he still had his doubts.

FOURTEEN
NOAH

It was a gorgeous morning, with the sun shining through the trees, and the forest brilliant with autumn's vivid colors. It had been a great weekend with Audrey, first with the Explorers on Saturday, and then just her and me on Sunday.

I'd taken her to my favorite spot in the forest. We laid out a blanket by the stream for a picnic. We were briefly visited by a mother deer and her fawn. The young deer was almost fully grown now, but still learning from its mother. It stared at us with black eyes that were like liquid pools before disappearing into the brush.

Best of all, Audrey and I made love under the trees, and then again in my cabin, and once more this morning.

"Are you sure you have to go to work?" I teased, not wanting to let her go.

"I'm sure. Besides, don't you have things to do today?"

"Nah, I'm a mountain man, living wild and free. I go wherever nature takes me," I joked, but in reality, she was right. I did have a lot of work to do. Shenandoah Travel was keeping me busy with urban tourists eager to hike through the fall foliage, and I wanted to design a new route that would take them past the falcon's nest I'd spied when I was out with Audrey. The mated raptors were a beauty to behold when they flew through the skies, hunting prey for their babies. I knew the tourists would love it.

I walked with Audrey hand in hand from the cabin down to her car, then went to the lodge, where I found Sean sitting on the steps looking grim as hell.

"What's wrong? Somebody die?" I teased, but when Sean looked up at me, I wondered if maybe I'd just stuck my foot in my mouth.

"Yeah, we did," Sean said miserably. "Shenandoah Travel just called. They're canceling their contract. I managed to convince them to come here for an emergency meeting, but I don't see how we can talk our way out of this one."

"Why not? What's the reason they're canceling?" I could feel my muscles tense, ready to defend my business against any enemy. Even one that was supposed to be my ally.

"Take a look at this," Sean said, and handed me the newspaper he'd been holding.

Right there, big as life, was a full story entitled, "Endangered Salamander Poisoned to Death." It was an opinion piece written by Tom Darnell, who was the brother-in-law of none other than Paul Hathaway.

That son of a bitch!

My blood began to roil with rage as I read the article, calling out Pine Creek Lodge specifically by name, and falsely claiming we were destroying the habitat of the Shenandoah salamander with pollution and improper waste disposal. He basically eviscerated us, with no real facts to back up his claims, since it was purely an opinion piece.

Shit, I could wring his scrawny little neck if he were in arm's reach instead of safely at the newspaper office, protected by an army of lawyers waving the First Amendment in the air like a banner. I'd gone to war to protect our Constitution, and this was how I was repaid.

"This article is complete bullshit," I stated emphatically, as the board members of Shenandoah Travel sat across from me in their suits and ties later that day. They were all looking at me like I was some kind of fucking monster, and it was taking all my willpower not to act like one.

"Stay calm, Noah," Sean said carefully. I'd been practicing my calm voice all morning, but as soon as I saw their faces and the way they'd already condemned me, I could feel myself losing my temper.

"I'm sorry, but they need to know this article is based on local politics and not facts. It's pure lies written by a relative of our biggest rival. You've toured every inch of this lodge, have you seen any evidence of improper waste disposal or pollution?" I growled, barely keeping my cool intact.

"It doesn't matter that the article has no merit," one of the board members said haughtily. "Negative public perception alone is enough to void the contract. We can't be associated with facilities with this kind of bad reputation. It brings down the integrity of our business."

That did it. I wasn't holding back any longer.

"You guys are fucking cowards."

I saw Sean bury his face in his hands as I blew my fuse. I knew I was out of line, but I couldn't help it. Being falsely accused, and then punished for an offense I didn't commit, was a bigger injustice than I could tolerate.

Pointing an angry finger at each and every one of those bastards, I said angrily, "You should have the guts to stand up for what you know to be the truth. Pine Creek Lodge is a business dedicated to preserving nature and all the creatures of the forest. Your company obviously only cares about money, and is beneath ours. I'm canceling the contract with you, not the other way around."

I couldn't stand to be in that room with them for one more minute, and stormed outside the lodge. I charged through the trail where I could escape their prying eyes. I found my ax, and set myself to the task of chopping the large logs into smaller piles of firewood. We'd need that this winter, anyway.

Swinging the ax through the air helped burn off my hostile energy. There was something gratifying about feeling the ax bite through the wood that soothed my soul. Slowly I felt my blood pressure lower and the veins in my neck stopped throbbing. Still, I kept chopping just to keep myself occupied.

"Well, they're gone and they're probably never coming back." Sean sighed heavily when he came out about forty-five minutes later.

"I know. I'm sorry," I said, and meant it.

"I needed that monthly income," Sean said somberly. "I've been going over the books, and referrals from Shenandoah Travel amounted to more than half our clientele. Without them, we'll both have to take a drastic pay cut."

"I know," I said, staring down at my boots. I didn't need my income from this lodge to live on. I'd inherited more money from my parents than I could ever spend. Sean, on the other hand, needed it desperately. He had a wife and a mortgage, and now a baby on the way.

Part of the reason I made Sean a partner in the lodge instead of just hiring him to be an employee was because I wanted him to have more of a secure future for himself and his family. He may have had a business degree, but he was never going to make much money as a manager for some local business living in a small town like North Haven, and this was where his heart was.

Sean wasn't cut out to move to the big city and fight and claw his way up the corporate ladder. He was born in North Haven, and this was where he belonged, so I'd tried to provide for him by making him my partner. I figured half the profits of a successful lodge would allow him to live quite comfortably. I just forgot that the key word in that plan was *successful*. Now that we'd lost all the income from Shenandoah Travel, we'd be underwater in a matter of months.

"This is my fault." I tried to apologize, but I couldn't find the words.

"Don't beat yourself up," Sean comforted me. "They were going to pull out of the contract no matter what was said here today. They'd made up their minds to do that the moment they saw that damn opinion article."

"That's what I'm talking about. The article is my fault," I said, my stomach twisted in fucking knots from the guilt.

"You didn't write it," Sean said easily.

"No, but I'm the reason it was written. If Pine Creek Lodge had been owned by anybody but me, nobody would give a shit. Everyone in town would probably welcome the new business with open arms. But I'm a fucking Cole, and you know as well as I do what everybody in this town thinks of the Cole legacy. I barely even knew my father, but his crooked, greedy ways have branded me forever, and every-thing I do. This business is doomed to failure because I'm one of the Cole brothers."

"So, why not let that be your strength instead of your weakness?" Sean asked naively.

"What the fuck are you talking about?" I was annoyed, and yet curious.

"The Cole legacy isn't just having the townspeople hate you. It's also a legacy of wealth, success, influence, and power. You aren't alone in this town. You still have a family of four brothers who would do anything for you if you just asked."

"I doubt that." I rolled my eyes. "I haven't wanted anything to do with them in years, and I'm sure the feeling is mutual. We are brothers by genetics only. Other than that, they might as well be strangers."

"It doesn't have to be that way. You're the one who keeps pushing them away, not the other way around," Sean dared to say, and I could feel my muscles getting tense again.

"This isn't really any of your business," I growled low, and I saw Sean take a step back, remembering the last time he pissed me off about shit that wasn't any of his concern.

"Actually, it is my business," Sean said bravely, but from a safe distance. "The Pine Creek Lodge is my business. We're partners, remember? And I say if we can get your brothers to help fix this mess we're in, then we need to ask. If you won't talk to them, then I will."

"It takes balls to speak to me that way," I said low, looking Sean up and down, trying to decide how to react.

"I know. Usually you're the one who commits all the acts of bravery around here, but if you're too chickenshit to talk to your brothers, then I guess I have to step up and do it."

"No. If anyone's going to ask my brothers for help, it should be me. But I don't want to make a habit of running to them every time I'm in trouble."

"I don't think anyone would ever accuse you of that,"

Sean assured me with a smile. "Then again, they did accuse you of polluting the salamander's habitat, so I guess anything is possible."

Sean looked nervous as hell, wondering how I'd react, but his joke was funny and so I grabbed him by the neck, ruffled his hair playfully.

"I'll tell you what's possible!" I laughed heartily, from deep in my gut. It felt good to release the tension of the day, and I really did admire Sean for having the guts to stand his ground against me. My little nerd was growing up.

Now it was my turn to man up and face my brothers.

FIFTEEN
AUDREY

"I can cancel the trip," Noah said gruffly, giving me a worried look.

"Don't be ridiculous," I said, as I helped hold closed the flaps of his overstuffed backpack while he cinched the straps down tight. It looked like he was going camping for three weeks instead of just three days. Wagging a chastising finger at him, I said, "The lodge can't afford for you to just cancel on clients at the last minute. Now take those folks from Roanoke on their guided camping trip and show them the forest in the way that only you can. Who knows, if you impress them, they might book you for big corporate retreats, where the big money is at. We city slickers are like that."

"Sean could take them without me. He's done it before," Noah said weakly, and I just rolled his eyes at him and he was forced to admit that would be a disaster. It was a group of six adult couples who'd never been camping before, and they'd chosen Pine Creek Lodge specifically for Noah's expertise. If he wasn't their guide, they'd no doubt just cancel.

"All right, so maybe Sean can't do it without me. I just feel weird being completely out of contact range for three whole days when we don't know if your creepy ex is still out there or not," Noah confessed.

I comforted him with a kiss and said, "I appreciate that, but no one's seen or heard from Wayne in days. He's probably moved on to torment the next town. Aren't you the one who told me I can't let him stop me from living my life the way I want to?"

"I am," Noah admitted begrudgingly.

"Well, the same goes for you too. You love being in the woods and showing rich, paying city slickers what's truly great and beautiful about nature. So, get out there and do what you love. I'll be perfectly fine here for the weekend. I'm a big girl, I can handle being alone for a few days."

"All right. If you're sure." Noah stared deep into my eyes, trying to determine if I was telling the truth or just putting on a brave front. I must have convinced him, because he gave me a long, passionate kiss goodbye, stroking my cheek as he did so. Then he left for the lodge, where Sean was waiting with the rich clients from Roanoke.

As much as I hated to see him go, I could make the most of his absence with some me time. I started with some yoga and a good run, enjoying how good it felt to stretch my muscles and breathe in the fresh air. Then I called the girls and invited them over for a special lunch prepared by the chef at the lodge. It had been far too long since I'd had a gossip session with my girlfriends and I had so much to tell them.

"This place is stunningly gorgeous. The views are breathtaking," Bethany gaped, trying to take it all in.

"Yeah, too bad the most breathtaking view of all has

gone camping for three days," Lauren chimed in, still as man-hungry as ever.

"Oh, stop!" Elisa shushed her. "Can't you tell Noah Cole is off the market? I think there's really something there between those two."

All eyes turned to me for confirmation, and I felt my cheeks turn bright pink.

"I don't know," I sputtered. "I do really like him, and I can tell he really cares about me. It's just seeing Wayne again really freaked me out, and it's hard to think about being in a new relationship with my old boyfriend still stalking me."

"We can all understand that," Elisa assured me. "But I think you're safe now. He must have left town. Nobody's seen him for days."

"That doesn't mean he's gone," I said. "Wayne's a lot craftier than people realize. He hid outside the private school where I worked for a week, learning the routines of the janitorial staff, as well as the access codes to the building. Then he broke in, hid in the vents of my classroom and recorded videos of me."

"How creepy!"

The girls looked horrified on my behalf, and once again I marveled at how good it felt to have real friends I could confide in. I couldn't tell these things to Noah, or he would have canceled his trip, and he needed the business. Besides, what if I was wrong and Wayne really was gone? Then I would have ruined Noah's business trip for nothing. It was better if I just kept my worries from him.

As the evening drew near and it was time for my friends to leave, Elisa invited me to sleep over at her house, but I declined. "No thanks. I've actually been looking forward to a night home alone."

"Yeah, so you can snoop through all his things, I know," Elisa teased. "Let me know if you find anything juicy in his diary."

"I will," I promised. I hugged the girls goodbye and watched as they all drove away from the lodge. The kitchen staff had left by then, and it was up to me to lock the lodge up and put out the closed sign.

Then I took my flashlight and walked up the trail from the lodge to the cabin I now shared with Noah. It was such an isolated little building, surrounded by nothing but trees. It gave it a certain charm, especially when compared to the noise and crowds of the city. I saw a rabbit nibbling on some grass, and it hopped away as I drew near, showing off its adorable white cottontail. I decided I much preferred this simple life up in the mountains.

Completely alone in the cabin for the evening, I was finally free to really look around and take in all the details without having to worry about Noah catching me snooping. He was such a quiet man, sometimes the best way to learn about him was by observation, rather than conversation. Although he had opened up to me quite a bit about his childhood, all his stories ended there. He didn't like to talk about anything past his parents' accident. I knew almost nothing about his life during or after the Marine Corps, or his relationship with his brothers now that they were grown.

As I looked around, I noticed all the furniture was made of beautifully handcrafted wood. I'd found out recently that the pieces had been made by his brother Owen, but Noah never talked about him. There was a single photo of Noah with his brothers, happy and smiling at his high school graduation. They all looked so close. I couldn't imagine why Noah had become estranged from them, and I was afraid to ask. Somehow, the personal subject felt taboo, and I stayed far away from mentioning it, although I was dying to know.

The clothes inside Noah's dresser were all folded neatly, military style, and the bed was always made so well, you could literally bounce a quarter off it. The dishes were always washed, never left sitting dirty in the sink, unless I'd set one there, and the floor was always swept and mopped. Noah kept his home in pristine military condition. Every day, he was up at dawn doing his chores, while he let me sleep late, cozy in the bed we shared.

The books on his shelf were fictional thrillers. The man liked his action stories. The pictures on his walls were of military men looking smart in their uniforms, ready to serve their country. The medal hung neatly in a fancy frame was the Gold Lifesaving Medal. Oddly enough, it was the only frame in the cabin that was covered in dust, as if he didn't want to look at it, or didn't feel like he deserved it. Everything else in the cabin was immaculate, without a speck of dust anywhere.

The one thing Noah was lacking was a television. I hadn't really missed it before, since we spent all our evenings together doing *other* recreational activities, but now that I was home alone for the weekend, its absence left me feeling kinda bored.

I decided to indulge in one of my favorite me time activities. I filled the tub with steaming hot water, added some lavender-scented bath beads, lit some candles, poured a glass of wine, and slipped into heaven.

God, it felt so good just to soak in the hot water, breathing in the calming scent of lavender and just relaxing. Soft music played from my iPod, and I decided to sample one of Noah's detective novels.

I usually only read romance stories, but this murder

mystery was actually quite good. I quickly got lost in the suspense, as my toes turned into little prunes in the water and my bath beads slowly dissolved into nothing.

A tapping sound outside the window made me jump. It was probably just the trees blowing in the evening breeze, but it made me realize reading a suspense novel when I was home alone in an isolated cabin in the woods might not be the best idea.

I was just preparing to climb out of the tub, when suddenly the power went out.

My heart started to pound, and I suddenly felt a chill.

Thank God I'd lit some candles or I'd have been plunged into complete darkness. Still, it scared the crap out of me.

Naked and alone, I fumbled for a towel, tripping on the clothes I'd left discarded on the floor and losing my balance. One of my candles fell into the tub, lowering the minimal light even further.

"Crap!" I muttered.

I treated the remaining candle like a fragile treasure as I searched the cabin for a flashlight, lantern, or even more candles.

"What kind of mountain man doesn't have supplies for a power outage?" I muttered under my breath when I came up emptyhanded.

I saw my cell phone sitting on the bed and I grabbed it like a lifeline. I could call Elisa and she'd be here to pick me up in a matter of minutes, but that suddenly felt so foolish. I was an independent city chick. How would it look if I went crying for help after just five minutes without power? I'd never live down the humiliation.

It was time to put my big girl panties on and act like the mature, street-savvy, capable woman I was. I got dressed quickly, slipped on my boots, and used my phone to look up what to do in case of a power outage. The first thing on the list was to check the fuse box.

Could it really be that simple? God, I hoped so! Thinking that it might be as easy as flipping a switch filled me with a sense of hope and relief. I couldn't find the fuse box inside, so I went outdoors to look for it.

The moon was in its dark phase, and I was surprised by just how black the night was without it. The sound of leaves rustling under my boots seemed extra loud in the dead silence of the night, and a creepy feeling washed over me, like I was being watched.

"No more murder mystery novels for me ever again," I chastised myself as I crept forward along the side of the cabin, searching for the fuse box.

I saw something glinting, and I shone my phone's flashlight upon it. Relief flooded through me as I realized it was the metal fuse box. Thank God I'd found it!

The leaves crunched under my feet as I ran up to it. But when I came to a stop, I could have sworn I heard the rustling sound continue for just a second somewhere in the woods nearby.

"Is someone there?" I turned the flashlight into the open wilderness, staring into the blackness beyond the trees, straining my eyes to see. My heart was pounding in my chest, and my legs were trembling, eager to flee.

Suddenly, a terrifying thought occurred to me, and I called out frightfully, "Wayne? Is that you?"

My throat seemed to close as I listened, but no answer came.

Moving quickly, I pried open the fuse box. Indeed, the breakers for the cabin were switched off. I turned them back on, and instantly light flowed through the windows of the cabin, warm and bright. I'd never felt so relieved in my life, and yet I couldn't shake that feeling that I wasn't out of the dark yet. Someone was out there, watching me.

Slamming the fuse box shut, I ran as fast as I could around the cabin, back through the door. I shut it firmly behind me, turned the deadbolt, and leaned against it, feeling breathless.

My phone was still in my hand. Suddenly, it started ringing, and I screamed aloud, nearly dropping it before answering it with a cautious "Hello?"

"Hey, how's the life of a single woman?" It was Elisa.

"Good," I lied. "I was just taking a bath and reading a book."

"Nice!" Elisa said. "I wanted to check on you in case you changed your mind about being alone out there."

"Thanks, but I'm perfectly fine," I lied.

For some reason I just couldn't bring myself to tell her that I was utterly terrified. I had no proof that Wayne had turned off the breakers in the fuse box, but I couldn't deny the possibility that he might have. Still though, I didn't want to be a pathetic city girl who jumped and cried wolf at every noise in the forest.

I chatted with Elisa for a bit, until my nerves calmed and we eventually hung up. Then I was all alone.

I lay hidden under the covers, clutching my cell phone and counting the hours until Noah returned home and I'd be safe in his arms again.

SIXTEEN

NOAH

"Next time I book a three-day excursion with six couples from the city, just shoot me." Sean groaned as he got into my truck. The clients were in a van behind us, following us slowly down the mountain back towards the lodge, singing campfire songs, and feeling exhausted but happy.

"Aw, come on," I laughed, ruffling the top of Sean's head. "They weren't that bad."

"Not that bad?" Sean looked at me like I was crazy. "Even *I* know how you have to stake down your tent on level ground. When that guy insisted on pitching his tent on that grassy slope because it would be more comfortable, I knew he'd wake up in the morning with a headache, and of course I was right, but would he listen? No, of course not. Because we were ignorant country hicks and he was a CEO at Dickhead Incorporated."

"Damn, Sean, tell me how you really feel."

I couldn't stop laughing. Usually Sean was the one keeping me from blowing my temper, not the other way around. It was kinda fun seeing him riled up for a change. I didn't know he had it in him.

Clasping him on the shoulder, I said, "The income from this weekend pulled us out of the red for this month, and into the black. And you have to admit, it was pretty damn funny when none of them knew how to tie a simple figure eight knot."

"You were surprisingly patient teaching them," Sean noted.

"I have Audrey to thank for that," I said, passing the compliment to the one who truly deserved it.

"You mean she couldn't tie a figure eight either?" Sean misunderstood, or maybe he was teasing me with that dry nerdy wit of his. Sometimes it was hard for me to tell.

"No, I mean she taught me how to connect with my clients the same way she does with her students when she's teaching. Audrey never lets the little things get to her. She just uses them as a way to better relate with the kids. I used to get so frustrated with people, but Audrey's helped me to be a better wilderness guide and a better businessman. She just makes me want to be kinder, more patient, and even friendlier to everyone."

"Who are you and what have you done with my partner?" Sean teased.

"Fuck you." I gave him a playful shove that nearly knocked his scrawny frame into the door. Sean shoved me back, and we both laughed like brothers.

"You're really beginning to like this girl, aren't you?" Sean asked thoughtfully after a few moments.

"Obviously," I said with a sarcastic edge. "I don't usually sleep with women I don't like."

"No, I mean Audrey is more than just a sexual fling, isn't she? You really like her. She's become someone you can talk to and share ideas with. But she's more than a friend, she's a real girlfriend."

"Shut up! Fuck you!" I snapped, but Sean wasn't buying the tough guy act.

"You've developed true feelings for her," Sean said, confident in his nerdy analysis of me, and I knew there was no point in trying to deny it. "Does she feel the same way about you?"

"I don't know. We haven't really discussed it yet," I grumbled.

"Well, are you two in a monogamous relationship now? Does she consider herself to be your girlfriend? Is this something with a real future?"

"Stop trying to analyze everything!" I barked. "We haven't discussed any of that. So far I've just been going with the flow, not wanting to ruin the good thing I've got going here by accidentally saying the wrong thing and fucking it up."

"As long as you speak from your heart, you can never say the wrong thing," Sean advised.

"Bullshit," I snorted derisively. "Believe me, if anyone can fuck things up by saying the wrong thing, it's me. How do you think I have over half the town ready to lynch me? I like to blame it on my father's legacy, but if I'm being honest, a lot of the animosity folks feel toward me is because of the way I've treated people. The day I met Audrey, I insulted her. The only reason she ever spoke to me again was because you charmed her into letting us host that field trip for the kids. Otherwise, she'd still hate my fucking guts."

"Well, obviously you found a way to get on her good side," Sean said. "I may have helped open the door, but I certainly didn't make her fall into bed with you. Something tells me she likes you just as much you like her."

"How do I know for sure?"

"You just have to man up and ask her. Do what I did when I asked Jenna to go steady."

"Do you live in the 1950s?" I cut him off with a mocking snort. "Nobody's used the phrase 'going steady' since my grandmother was a kid!"

"Hey, who's the one here who married the girl of his dreams and who's the one who might end up all alone if he doesn't take some good advice?" Sean fired back at me. I realized the nerd was right, and I'd better listen to him.

I sat up straighter, as Sean laid out his plan.

"Make her a nice dinner, with wine and candles, and the whole works. Tell her how you feel about her. Speak from the heart. Then shut up and give her a chance to tell you how she feels. Don't pressure her or try to put words in her mouth. Just shut up and listen. That's the key to any good relationship, listening."

"I think I can handle that," I said as we pulled up to the lodge.

"Good," Sean grinned, "because she's here."

The moment I climbed out of the truck, Audrey came running down the path, and flung herself into my arms. God, she was beautiful, and she smelled so good and felt so soft. I didn't realize I'd missed her so much until she was in my arms again and I could feel her breasts pressed against my chest and her sweet mouth kissing mine.

Sean waved me off and said, "I'll take care of getting the clients checked out. You go ahead and catch up with Audrey. I have a feeling you two have a lot to talk about."

"Thanks," I said to Sean. Then I turned all my attention to Audrey, walking arm in arm with her up the trail back to the cabin.

"I missed you so much!" she said excitedly as I held her close to my side. I could feel her heart beating and I liked it.

"I missed you too," I said, surprised by just how happy I was to be with her again. I never wanted to leave her side. Squeezing her hand, I asked, "How were things here while we were gone?"

"Awful!" She broke down into tears, startling me. Shit! What did I do wrong?

I pulled her into my arms, holding her against my chest as I stroked her hair. "It'll be all right. I'm here now. I'll take care of everything."

Finally, Audrey's sobs slowed into soft hiccups. I found a bandana in my pocket and gave it to her so she could dry her eyes and blow her nose. I waited till we got all the way back to the cabin, and she was seated comfortably on the bed, then I asked her what happened.

"It was nothing really," she said, but I just gave her a look that said I didn't have time to play games. Taking a deep breath, she said, "I just feel so foolish. I don't have any proof that my suspicions are correct, and I might just be completely paranoid, but I know what my gut's telling me, and they say to always trust your instincts."

"Just stop and breathe." I put my arms around her gently, and took some deep breaths, encouraging her to do the same. "You're not making any sense. Just tell me what happened from the beginning."

I listened silently while Audrey told me the whole story of what she'd been through. She kept apologizing for being paranoid, but when I pressed her on the details, she was quite confident that her instincts were right.

"You weren't running any appliances?" I asked.

"No. Only my iPod, but that had been running the

entire time I was in the bath. I didn't suddenly turn anything on, the breakers just shut off."

"Well, it doesn't seem likely they would go out on their own for no reason. There were no storms that night? Bad weather? High winds?"

"No, it was a perfectly calm night. Just a light breeze, but not enough to affect the power."

"It sounds like you're sure," I said, and Audrey looked surprised.

Shaking her head, she said, "That's just it, I'm not sure Wayne's behind this at all. I never saw him and I have no proof he was there. It could have just been my imagination."

"But you're sure your gut was warning you of some impending danger, and you're sure there's no other cause for the power to have been switched off. That's all I need to know."

"Really? So you believe me?" Tears of emotion sprang to her big brown eyes, and I just wanted to hold her and protect her.

"I believe you, Audrey. If you tell me something wasn't right that night, then I'm going to do everything I can to secure this place to make sure it never happens again."

"So, you don't think I'm crazy?" She hugged me gratefully.

"Oh, you're crazy all right," I teased. Giving her a leering look, I kissed her passionately and said, "Crazy hot!"

Audrey leaned back on the bed and kissed me back. She started to strip off my clothes, but I forced myself to have restraint.

"Not until I do a complete security sweep of the area. I want to replace some lights with ones with motion sensors, and put up a whole new security camera system."

"But you just got back," Audrey gave me a sultry pout.

"Yeah, but I promised to protect you and keep you safe, and I already let you down. That'll never happen again," I vowed.

"I think I'm falling for you," Audrey called out spontaneously.

It made me stop mid-stride and I turned and stared at her. "What was that?"

She got up off the bed, walked across the room and put her delicate hands in mine. Looking up into my eyes, she smiled softly and said, "I'm falling for you."

I pulled her into my arms and kissed her, so long and hard, it stole her breath away. Then I let her go, flashed her a big grin and said, "I'm falling for you too."

As she stood there, breathless and smiling, I turned and walked out the door, more determined than ever to keep her safe.

"I can't believe you didn't call me! Or at least tell me you needed me when I called you!" Elisa was mad as hell Monday, when we were hanging out in my classroom at the end of the workday.

"I know. I'm sorry. I was just embarrassed and I didn't want to inconvenience you."

"Well, it would be a lot more inconvenient if I had to go to the morgue to identify your dead body, plus I would think it would be a lot more embarrassing for you."

"You're right, but obviously I didn't get killed and I'm perfectly fine."

"Well, the next time you won't be! Even if Wayne isn't stalking you, I'll kill you myself for not coming to me when you thought you were in trouble! Isn't that what best friends are for?"

"All right. I promise, if anything like that ever happens again, I'll call you right away."

"Damn straight!" Elisa nodded her head emphatically. Then she hugged me tight, and I knew she had forgiven me.

With a casual air, I said, "Just so you know, I doubt I'll

ever feel scared like that again. Noah put in a state-of-the-art security system all around the property, hidden in the trees and in the rocks. There are cameras and motion sensors and lights. If anyone sets foot on the property, it gets recorded and the live stream can be accessed by Noah on his cell phone, anywhere and anytime."

"It must be nice to have a wealthy former Marine protecting you like that," Elisa said wistfully, and I had to agree that it was. Suddenly, Elisa jerked her head towards the window of my classroom and said, "Speak of the devil, look who just pulled up outside."

"Noah! What are you doing here?" I ran out to greet him with a huge smile on my face.

"You said you got off work at 4:00 p.m., so I thought I'd surprise you."

Noah was dressed in new black jeans, shiny black boots, a blue button-down shirt, and even a tie with blue and black stripes.

"You look very nice," I said. I couldn't hide my delight.

"So do you," Noah complimented, taking in the sight of me in my simple form-fitting, cream-colored dress that stopped just above my knees, and a thin brown leather belt to accent my waist. My hair was pulled back in a ponytail and a pair of knee-high leather boots completed the look. When Noah looked at me that way, I felt like the most beautiful woman in the world, and I couldn't help but blush.

"So, what do you say, Miss Sawyer? Will you go on a date with me?" He held out his hand to me gallantly.

It suddenly occurred to me that we hadn't actually been on an official date yet. A huge smile spread across my face as I accepted his hand and he guided me into the passenger seat of his truck.

"Where are we going on this date?" I asked. I'd never seen this side of him before, and I was bubbling with curiosity.

"I'm going to show you the best of North Haven," Noah said with a sexy grin. "We'll start with the best golf course around."

"I'm afraid I don't know how to golf," I confessed, feeling like I'd already ruined his big plans.

"You've never played golf at all?" Noah sounded surprised, but not disappointed like I thought he might be.

"Well, not unless you count miniature golf." I giggled with chagrin. "My dad used to take me all the time when I was a kid, and I loved it. I can't remember the last time I played."

"In that case, you're in for a treat because Mother Goose Mini Golf is the best golf course in all of Southern Virginia."

I squealed with delight as Noah pulled his truck to a stop at the quaint little miniature golf resort, filled with giant plaster replicas of the Old Woman Who Lived in a Shoe, Humpty Dumpty's wall, and Bo Peep's sheep. My putting skills needed a lot more practice, as did his. We both went way over par on every hole, but we had the best time laughing and flirting.

By the time we were done, the sun had set and my stomach was beginning to rumble.

"Hungry?" Noah asked, and I nodded emphatically. "Good. Because next on the itinerary is North Haven's best restaurant."

"Let me guess, the diner?" I teased.

"Not even close. I might like to play like a kid, but my culinary tastes have gotten a lot more sophisticated since I was nine." Noah grinned sexily.

He drove nearly out of the town's limits, up a long, winding road to a beautiful building on a hilltop, looking out over the vast horizon.

"This is the Vista, the finest restaurant in North Haven, and pretty much anywhere I've been around the world."

It was an elegant restaurant, with tables arranged around the central, empty dance floor that looked like something out of a classic movie. I was surprised to see such fine dining in North Haven. Soft jazz played as patrons enjoyed their gourmet meals.

We were given a perfect table with a view of the stars shining over the valley like wishes waiting to be made. The brightly lit homes and shops below looked like a perfect little replica of some small town in a Norman Rockwell painting, and it made my breath hitch in my throat to see it that way.

Noah spared no expense on the meal, and it felt like we had the whole staff of waiters and waitresses to serve us exclusively. We started with a bottle of Cristal champagne. Then oysters and crab cakes for an appetizer, followed by a salad of wild greens. For our entrees, I had the rainbow trout cooked with winter vegetables and Noah had the rib-eye steak with potatoes and asparagus. The food was delicious—better than anything I'd ever had in Charlotte.

"Oh my God, please tell me dessert isn't coming next, because I can't eat another bite," I said, feeling quite full and more than a little tipsy. That Cristal definitely went to my head a lot faster than the cheap stuff I normally drank.

"Nope, not dessert. Will you dance with me?"

He stood up and held his hand out to me.

"What? Here?" I gaped, looking around at the empty dance floor of the restaurant surrounded by tables of people dining.

"It's the best dance floor in North Haven," Noah stated confidently.

"Isn't it the *only* dance floor in North Haven?" I asked, my eyes darting around at the other patrons. I wasn't much of a dancer. I could fake it in a crowded club, but to be the only couple dancing, with all eyes staring at me, I knew I'd make a fool of myself. There was no way I was going to let him talk me into doing it.

"Audrey, you're the most beautiful woman I've ever seen," he said, looking into my eyes. "Let me dance with you."

Damn it! Now I couldn't say no. With my heart pounding, I let Noah lead me out on the dance floor. I could feel all the eyes in the room boring into me, but I just kept my gaze on Noah and pretended no one else was there.

The next song began to play, and I moved my feet, awkwardly at first, but Noah was surprisingly skilled as a dance partner. All I had to do was look into his eyes and let him lead me where the music wanted us to go. When the song was done, we actually got a round of applause from the rest of the diners, and I took a shy curtsy.

After that, more diners abandoned their tables to join us on the floor, and we spent the night dancing like I hadn't done since I was a kid in college, hitting the clubs at night. It felt fun, freeing, and magical.

"I can't remember the last time I had so much fun," I sighed happily as I limped to our table to give my feet a rest.

"I guess I should have warned you to wear comfortable shoes," Noah said apologetically.

"It's okay. These are actually my most comfortable pair," I said. "But I think we better call it quits for the night if I'm going to be able to walk out of here."

"I agree," Noah said. I saw him leave a very generous tip

as he paid the bill, and then he extended his arm for me to lean on as I hobbled to his truck.

As we drove toward home, I yanked my boots off. My feet quickly felt better, but I felt a pang of guilt.

"I'm sorry to ruin the evening," I apologized.

"You didn't. Not at all." Noah flashed me his most charming smile.

"I know you had more on your list of the best of North Haven that we still hadn't gotten too, and now I've ruined your plans."

"I wouldn't say that," Noah assured me. He pulled the truck up to the end of a dead-end road and rolled to a slow stop at the edge of a plateau. It looked down on a perfect view of the area below, looking absolutely breathtaking in the wilderness.

"I see the lodge!" I gasped, pointing excitedly.

"Yeah, you can see the whole valley from up here. Everything seems so perfect from this spot. It's definitely the best view in North Haven."

"I would have to agree." I grinned. Beyond the lodge, the small town was lit up against the darkness. I located the middle school, the cluster of shops downtown, and other landmarks.

"Who lives there?" I asked, pointing to an elegant house on the near edge of the town. "In that huge house right on the lake?"

Noah paused for a moment that seemed to stretch on forever.

"I used to, along with my family," Noah said. "It's the house I grew up in."

"Wow," I said. "It looks really nice from here. And it's right on the lake, with so much land surrounding it. It must have been great growing up there. Lots of room for kids to run around."

Noah nodded his head. "It had its perks."

"Who lives there now?"

"My brother Gavin," Noah said, staring off at the house with its windows lit up.

"Oh," I said, unsure of what to say. It was the first time Noah had ever mentioned one of his brothers by name.

"He's the brother just older than me," Noah said. "He runs my dad's business, and he was the only one who wanted our family home."

"Do you see your brothers much?" I asked.

He shook his head, tightening his jaw. "Not really. They're a bunch of assholes."

I raised my eyebrows, surprised by his response.

He ran a hand through his thick brown hair. "Okay, so that's a little harsh. But I keep my distance from them."

I turned to face him. "Do you not get along with them?"

"Well, it's more complicated than that," Noah said.

"Do you want to tell me about it?"

He took a deep breath. As I listened attentively, he finally revealed to me the circumstances of his parents' death—including the guilt he still felt.

"Wow. I had no idea. I'm so sorry," I said, feeling shocked. I couldn't imagine how difficult it must have been to not only lose his parents at such a young age, but then to also carry the burden of feeling responsible for their deaths.

I wanted to tell him it wasn't his fault, that he wasn't responsible, but I knew he wouldn't respond well.

"After our parents died, my brothers never understood what I was going through. They kept telling me I wasn't to blame, when I knew the truth. I got so sick of them always pushing me toward therapy and the self-forgiveness bullshit. It was always the same conversation, so eventually I just quit talking to them as much. I guess we drifted apart over the years. And when I got back from Afghanistan..."

His voice trailed off.

"What?" I asked.

He cleared his throat. "I just wanted to be alone."

"I understand," I said, nodding, wishing I could take his pain away. "Do you miss them?" I asked.

Noah stared silently out at the valley for a long time. Then finally he said quietly, "Sometimes."

"When was the last time you saw your brothers?"

"I'm not sure. They tried to see me when I got back home over a year ago, but I made it clear I didn't want anything to do with them. I couldn't tell you the last time we really talked. It must have been before I enlisted, over eight years ago."

"So it's been nearly a decade since you talked with the only family you have left?" I said softly. Squeezing his hand, I asked, "Don't you think it's been long enough?"

"Maybe," Noah said, staring out at the night sky.

"You've been through so much. I'm so sorry," I said, caressing his face. "Thanks for telling me about this. I'm honored you wanted to share your past with me."

He gave me a slight smile. "I don't know why I'm bringing up all this old shit right now."

His eyes looked sad, and I realized he was done discussing it for now. I felt a little bad I'd brought up such a heavy topic for him. A date was supposed to be fun, and up until I started asking such personal questions, it had been.

Now it was time for me to liven it back up again.

I kissed him tenderly. Even as my heart broke for him over the tragic loss of his parents, I felt even closer to him than ever before. We had a unique bond now because he had shared such a personal part of himself with me when he didn't have to.

"You know, I had a really good time tonight. Thanks for showing me the best of North Haven," I whispered low in his ear.

I could see the tiny hairs stand up on his neck from my breath, and I took the opportunity to nibble his earlobe, making him shiver with desire. Unbuttoning his jeans, I pulled down his zipper and said, "I want you to have as good a time tonight as I did."

Noah closed his eyes and groaned with pleasure as I freed his manhood from his jeans and enveloped him with my hot, wet mouth. Within moments he was fully erect, and I lavished all of my attention on his hard cock, licking and sucking while he moaned loudly with pleasure. I loved making him feel this way. Now that he'd shared so much of himself, I wanted to reciprocate the emotional intimacy with physical intimacy.

"That feels amazing!" Noah groaned as he wrapped my ponytail around his hand, encouraging me to keep going harder and faster, until he was ready to explode. Then he drew my head back and said breathlessly, "You'd better stop. I'm getting way too hot."

"That's the way I like it," I purred. "Getting you hot makes me wet. Feel for yourself."

I wriggled my dress over my hips and pulled it off over my head so I was just in my bra and panties while Noah stared with excited disbelief. Then I took his hand and slid it inside my silk panties. Noah's eyes dilated as he discovered how moist I was.

"You're dripping," he moaned as he plunged a finger inside me, flicking my clit with his thumb. "Fuck, Audrey, you're sexy."

I gripped the dashboard of the truck, moaning and gasping with pleasure as Noah rubbed me until I came. My cries of intense joy filled the small cab of his truck as his fingers kept my orgasm going and going.

"I want you inside me," I panted, and I tore off my panties completely to get them out of the way. Finding the right position in the confined space of his truck was tricky, but we were both so horny, we didn't care. We needed each other, so we found a way to make it work.

When I felt Noah enter my tight, dripping entrance with his throbbing erection, it was pure heaven. I rocked my hips to meet him thrust for thrust till we both exploded in orgasm together, clutching and writhing with ecstasy as we rode intense waves of pleasure.

"You feel so amazing," Noah panted as our climaxes ebbed away, and we could finally talk and breathe again. "I love you, Audrey."

I felt tears of joy spring to my eyes to hear those words. I knew I felt the same about him.

"I love you, too, Noah."

And I truly meant it with all my heart.

He took me home to his cabin, where he made love to me again, sending me into realms of ecstasy I'd never before visited. After the sex, we cuddled together until my eyes grew heavy. I was bursting with happiness to be with Noah, and he made me feel safer than I had in a long time.

But despite my contentment, despite everything Noah had done to keep me safe, my dreams that night were filled with fear.

EIGHTEEN
NOAH

Two months later

It was an absolutely gorgeous day with the winter sun reflecting off the freshly fallen snow. I couldn't help but whistle a little tune as I spread ice melt along the pathway leading to the lodge and up the steps.

Several of the boards had come loose. I'd have to fix them before someone got hurt. Upon closer inspection, I noticed the nails had been pulled out of the boards. This wasn't regular wear from age, this was something more.

I doubted it was that asshole Wayne. No one had seen or heard from him in months. It was probably just some kids messing around. It was a shame I had the security cameras aimed on the doors and not the steps.

Still, I was in too happy a mood to let anything bring me down. After making love to Audrey last night, and then again this morning before breakfast, how could I not be?

I fixed the boards quickly, then finished sprinkling what was left of the ice melt on the porch, singing under my breath while I worked.

"You're in a good mood this morning," Sean commented as I entered the lodge, being mindful to knock the snow off my boots onto the doormat and not the hardwood floors.

"It's a fantastic day outside. Get off that damn computer and go enjoy it!" I grabbed Sean around the neck in a maneuver that was half wrestling, half brotherly hug. After kissing the top of his nerdy head, I let him go with a grin. "So, what's on the agenda today, partner?"

"Another full roster," Sean said happily, indicating his computer screen. "You've got a snowshoeing class this morning, a winter survival class after lunch, the Explorers this afternoon, and I just took a reservation for a group from the city who want to hike up to the summit for some stargazing tonight."

"When it rains, it pours," I said in mock complaint, but inside I was thrilled. Business was really booming, despite having lost the contract with Shenandoah Travel. The lodge was turning into a true success. Sean didn't know it yet, but he was going to be getting a very healthy bonus check for Christmas as a reward for all his hard work. Not to mention the trust fund I had created for the baby, so he or she would be guaranteed the chance to go to college.

"I can take the hikers up to look at the stars tonight." Sean surprised me by volunteering for the gig.

"Are you sure?"

"Yeah, it's an easy trail and Jenna loves stargazing. She exercises every day to keep fit for the baby, so I know she'll be able to keep up. Besides, she says we need to squeeze in as much quality time together as we can before the baby comes."

"I don't think tagging along with you at work is what she has in mind," I warned.

"All right, Mr. Know-It-All. What do you do to keep the romance alive?" Sean turned the tables on me.

"Well, for starters, I haven't been married for years like you have, but if we had, I'd probably keep doing what I've been doing. Going on long hikes together, talking over dinner, and keeping each other warm under the sheets at night."

"I see." Sean made that expression he always made when he was mocking me, but thought I was too much of a jock to figure it out.

"What's wrong with that?" I glared in mock hostility, even though he knew I was kidding.

"In a relationship, you need to work to keep the romance alive," Sean said. "Plan romantic activities, do things that make her feel special, let her know she's the only woman for you. It might not sound romantic to you, but I know Jenna will love it when I hold her by the hand and we gaze up at the stars tonight, and make a wish together. It's those kinds of gestures that keep a woman from feeling taken for granted, and once that happens, that's when you lose her."

"Thanks, but I think we're doing okay." I scoffed, thinking of the hot sex Audrey and I had just had last night. Well, actually last night was just a quickie because we were both tired, but the night before I had gone all out in the romance department. Actually, the night before had been a quickie too. I guess it was last week that I'd really made her feel special, with candles and music and her favorite wine. Or was it the week before? Aw, shit! Maybe Sean was right. Maybe I was letting the romance slip away.

I couldn't get my mind off it. All the while as I was teaching seniors how to snowshoe, I kept coming up with new ways to show Audrey just how much she meant to me, until finally I came up with the perfect idea.

"Okay, great class, everybody. I'll see you all next week." I clapped my hands and indicated for my students to turn in their gear.

"Is the hour over already?" Mr. Holland tried to look at his watch, but it was buried under layers of clothes and his gloves were too thick to move his sleeves.

"Absolutely. Time flies when you're having fun."

I collected all the snowshoes and poles and carried them to the supply shed with a spring in my step. I had a lot of work to do if I was going to plan this surprise in time for Audrey. She was going to love it. As I went to lock the shed, however, I stopped short. Someone had been messing with the lock. It had scratches and scrapes all over it, like someone inexperienced had been trying to pick it. I looked up and saw the security camera aimed at the door of the shed had been broken by rocks.

"Sean, call the fucking police," I shouted out as I stormed towards the lodge, only to run into none other than Paul Hathaway. Fucking great. My archrival was the last person I wanted to know we had a vandal screwing around on my property. He'd use the information to trash my business and build up his.

Paul stormed toward me and shouted, "I want to talk to you, Noah Cole!"

My good mood had been shattered like the broken lens of my security camera, and I had no patience for a hothead like Paul. Pushing past him, I glared. "Not now, Hathaway."

"Actually, now is the only time." Paul grabbed my arm. I was about to deck him for it when I saw his kid, Tyler, watching from inside his truck. I should have known he'd pull a disgusting maneuver like bringing his son along to witness this encounter. What a chickenshit move. Well, there was no way I was being goaded into a fistfight in front of the man's son.

"Fine, what do you want to talk about?" I asked through gritted teeth.

"Your appointment book is filled with my clients. I ran an ad for winter survival classes, and two days later you offered the same class for less money. You knew my clients would jump ship and go running to you. You did it on purpose."

"Hey, it's called free enterprise. If you don't like it, tough," I shrugged. "Now if that's all, I have work to do."

"That's not all. You can't steal clients from me then act like it's nothing. I demand you cancel the ads and stop offering the deal!" Paul was livid, and I felt my own temperature rising to match his.

"Listen, nobody tells me how to run my business," I growled low, my hands curling into tight fists despite my best efforts to keep calm.

Suddenly, Sean appeared between us. "Hey, guys. Let me interrupt this little discussion. Noah, your next class is waiting for you out by the start of the trail. Why don't you take care of them? Meanwhile, Mr. Hathaway, if you would please join me in my private office, I'm sure we could have a civilized discussion on the matters that concern you."

"Forget it! You've already shown your lack of integrity by stealing my clients. I'm not going to waste my time letting you blow smoke up my ass in some private office. You two can both fuck off!" Then both Paul and his son were gone.

"What got into him?" Sean asked with a relieved sigh, then he turned to me with concern. "Are you all right? You look ready to pop."

"I just need some time away." I rubbed my hands on my head and tried to regain my composure.

"Take a vacation," Sean suggested brightly.

"Yeah, right." I laughed without humor. "And leave you with all these clients? They'd eat you alive."

"It won't be so bad. I can teach the wilderness survival class. I've watched you do it plenty of times, and I've had plenty of practice as your demonstration volunteer. I can handle the Explorers too, as long as Elisa does most of the work. So go ahead, take some time off. You'll need it, because I'm taking off an entire month when Jenna has the baby."

"Thanks. You're a true friend." I gave Sean a one-armed hug that nearly popped his eyes from his sockets, but I couldn't help it. I really loved that little guy. "I'll take you up on your offer. I've got some reservations to make and some tickets to buy."

NINETEEN
AUDREY

It was my first Christmas away from my family, but I didn't mind as much as I thought I might. Mom and Dad had offered to fly me down to Charlotte for the holiday, but I declined. Wayne would be stalking them next if I showed up at their house, and I wanted to protect them. Though I hadn't heard from my ex in months, my gut told me that he still hadn't given up his search for me. I would have to lay low for a while.

Besides, if I couldn't be with my family, Christmas at North Haven was the next best thing one could hope for. After living my whole life in the city, I was finally getting to enjoy the small-town Christmas experience I'd always longed for as a little girl, and it was even better than I imagined.

The previous Saturday, the whole town of North Haven gathered in the town square for the tree lighting ceremony, then we all drank hot cocoa and sang carols. The streets were white with snow, and there were wreaths, silver bells, and boughs of holly everywhere. Children were making snowmen and everyone was cheerful and friendly.

It was like being in one of those black and white movies I always loved watching, only now I was getting to live it.

The last day of school before winter break, I threw a party for my students in the classroom. We frosted sugar cookies and watched *Elf*. By the end of the day, every desk was sticky with frosting, but the students were beaming with joy, or perhaps their eyes were just glassed over from the sugar rush. Either way, it was a terrific day, and I knew I would miss them during the break.

The best part of the day was going home to Noah in our sweet little cabin in the woods. Noah had cut down a small pine tree for me to decorate and I made the place homey with all the little touches I'd liked best growing up. I found an adorable nutcracker at the Christmas craft fair, as well as a nativity set carved of wood, and some beautiful hand-painted ornaments for the tree.

"The only things missing are stockings," I mused, as Noah and I sat cuddled together by the fire, sipping brandy and eggnog.

"I'd be afraid they'd catch fire," Noah joked. I noticed he'd been doing that a lot lately. Not exactly mocking Christmas traditions, but just making light of them as if they didn't matter to him. I knew he'd been invited to spend Christmas with his brothers, but he'd told them he was too busy. I decided not to push him on it.

"What's your favorite part of Christmas?" I asked him casually. The fire and the brandy both had me feeling cozy and relaxed. "Something from when you were growing up, or maybe when you were in the Marines?"

Noah looked thoughtful for a moment, then the intense look in his eyes morphed into sentimental joy. He smiled softly and said, "I always liked giving better than receiving. I had such a privileged childhood. Even after my parents died, my brothers and I were well provided for in their will. I never wanted or needed for anything, so holidays like Christmas never felt like a big deal. In the Marines, I got to see a whole different way of living that I never really knew existed. Everybody's aware of poverty, but seeing it first-hand is something else entirely. Passing out relief packages full of supplies and Christmas presents to the villagers was one of the most rewarding experiences of my life. To see the look on a child's face when they receive a new pair shoes for the first time really changes your perspective on life. That's why every year I make donations to charities. This world's so fucked up, it's the least I can do."

"I had no idea you did that." I wiped away the tear that had fallen on my cheek. Suddenly, I felt the need to kiss him, but he held up a finger, stopping me.

"Speaking of giving, I have something for you." He reached into his pocket and pulled out an envelope.

"But it's not Christmas for three more days." I hesitated.

"Just open it," Noah insisted, and so I did.

My heart was pounding as I removed a letter and two tickets. It took me a moment to register what I was seeing, even as I read it. Then I squealed and dropped them all so I could wrap my arms around his neck and kiss him happily.

"You're taking me skiing in Switzerland for Christmas! I can't believe it! Thank you so much!" I smothered him in kisses, until suddenly I realized I had to stop and pack if we were going to make our flight on time.

Before I knew it, I was swooshing down the slopes of Zermatt, atop one of the most breathtaking mountain ranges in the world. Noah went first class all the way, with a luxurious suite in a chalet overlooking the Matterhorn itself. There was fine dining, gourmet chocolates, and one afternoon we even skied into Italy for lunch, literally doubling the number of foreign countries I'd ever been to in just one day.

"I can't believe tonight is our last night," I sighed when we got back to our hotel room. "Monday, it'll be back to reality, me with my lesson plans and you with your city slickers."

"Yeah, but I think it's a pretty damn good life," Noah said contentedly. He looked so sexy in that moment, it suddenly reminded me of something. We'd been so busy I nearly forgot all about it.

Standing up, I rummaged through my suitcase and found it in the little zippered compartment where I'd hidden it.

"Before we go, I need to give you my Christmas gift to you." I smiled salaciously, hiding it behind my back.

"You didn't need to get me anything," Noah practically groaned. "All I wanted for Christmas was just to spend time with you."

"I know. That's why I think you'll really like what I got you." I grinned. "Just let me put it on!"

I ran into the bathroom and locked the door. It took me a bit to figure out all the hooks and straps, but when I admired the finished product in the full-length bathroom mirror, I knew Noah would be pleased.

The Christmas-red corset was made of alternating panels of satin and lace and lined with a soft down of fur at the cleavage. Red satin garters attached to black fishnet stockings resting high up my thigh. The red satin thong was so tiny, it practically wasn't there. I slipped into a pair of three-inch stiletto heels and put a Santa hat on my head to complete the look. Dressed as a deliciously naughty elf, I'd never felt so sexy, yet I had a twinge of nervousness just before I opened the door. Would he like it or would he laugh?

"Merry Christmas, Noah," I purred as I presented myself to him. The look on Noah's face, followed by the immediate bulge forming in his slacks, removed any doubts I had over whether he'd like me or not.

I crossed the room slowly, with a sensual sway of my hips, and pushed him down on the bed.

"Tonight, you don't need to do a thing. Just lie back, and enjoy my gift to you," I said as I pulled the Santa hat off my head and placed it on his.

Noah rested back comfortably on the pillows as I stripped away his clothes and tossed them to the floor. I delighted in caressing his well-muscled body with my hands, scratching him with my nails, and titillating him with kisses as his naked flesh was exposed. His skin rippled as his muscles flexed, wanting more, and I felt myself growing wet.

Once he was completely naked, I stretched my body over his and began to kiss him sensuously. I started with his mouth, then his neck, then slowly worked my way down his torso, nipping at his nipples, and tickling his abs. Finally, I came to his pelvis. Noah sucked in a gasp of air as I spread his thighs, giving me full access to his balls in addition to his massive cock.

I took my time, giving my attention to every inch of him there. My tongue lapped and flicked and flitted. I opened my jaw wide as I took him deep in my throat, my hands cupping his balls. All the while Noah writhed and groaned in ecstasy over the pleasures I was giving him.

"God, that feels so good!" he kept moaning. His hands

wound through my hair, lightly tugging, and his muscles kept flexing as he gritted his teeth and groaned aloud, trying desperately not to come.

It was thrilling to be the one to make him feel that way. I liked knowing that I had that kind of power over him, and that I alone could bring him to such heights of pleasure. My thighs were dripping wet with the juices of my own sexual excitement by the time I started to strip off my lingerie so he could enter me.

"Wait," Noah stopped me. "It's my present. Let me be the one to unwrap it."

He wasted no time, ripping off the lingerie it had taken me so long to put on, removing it quickly in his eagerness. The moment I was naked, he filled his hands with my flesh, desperate to hold and touch me. He pulled me to him, and plunged into me powerfully, unable to hold back anymore. I was already so ready, the feel of him entering me was like a relief, and I sighed openly.

"I want you to fuck me," I panted, and Noah willingly obliged. Pounding into me, his thrusts had an urgency we both felt inside. I raised my hips, meeting him thrust for thrust, driving him deeply into me. He came quickly, but so did I, crying out to the ceiling as he brought me to heaven and back down again. Afterwards, we kept kissing and fondling each other, and I was amazed at how soon he was ready to go again.

The second time was sweeter and more tender. We took our time to enjoy kissing each other as we made love, and our orgasms were somehow stronger and even more powerful than they'd been the first time. Afterwards, we stretched out across the king-sized bed, naked and gooey, and smiling contentedly. I didn't think two people had ever been more satisfied or in love.

"So, did you have a good Christmas?" I asked Noah with a teasing wink.

"The very best I've ever had," Noah said emphatically, then sealed it with a kiss. "How about you?"

I thought about it for a moment. Christmas when I was growing up had always been filled with family but there had also been a lot of stress. This Christmas with Noah had been nothing but pure relaxation and enjoyment. And it wasn't just because we were staying in a luxury suite in the Swiss Alps and dining in restaurants with three Michelin stars, although all that had certainly been nice. What had made this Christmas special was the time I'd spent with a man I truly loved, who made me feel loved and appreciated in return.

Noah had gone out of his way to make sure I had the best Christmas of my life, and he'd succeeded. Wayne had never made me happy, and I couldn't imagine any other man on Earth could. When I was with Noah, I felt truly seen and heard, and that was more than I could say about the time I spent with my own family sometimes.

Kissing Noah tenderly, with all the love I felt in my heart, I said simply, "Me too."

"Good," Noah winked. "Because Monday it's back to reality."

I groaned in mock misery, but in truth, that wasn't so bad either. In fact, daily life with Noah was pretty damn terrific. I could be content living with him just like we were in his little cabin in the woods forever. I just hoped nothing ever happened to change what we had.

TWENTY
NOAH

Four months later

"I'll never forgive you for this!" Audrey shouted up at me as she was clinging to the side of the cliff, but the tone her voice made it clear she was only teasing.

"I know you love it," I grinned down at her, teasing her back. I pulled the slack tighter on her rope so she felt more secure, and shouted down, "This is the toughest part of the climb, but you can do it. Just raise your right foot up about eighteen inches to that toehold there. That will give you the leverage you need to reach up with your left hand and grab the next ledge."

"I did it!" Audrey cried out in victory.

She was beaming with pride, and I was glad she was having such a great time. I wanted our six-month anniversary to be special, and there was nothing more exhilarating than mountain climbing out in the open air.

Today was the first really warm spring day after what had been a long and wet winter. Luckily, Audrey and I had each other to keep each other warm, living up in my cabin.

Even after it was clear her ex-boyfriend Wayne had left town, Audrey had opted not to move back into her cottage. Instead, she canceled the rental and stayed with me. It was hard to believe we'd been living together as a couple for six whole months now.

"Is it much further?" Audrey puffed from below. I'd taken the lead on the climb so I could place our anchor cams and pick the easiest route up the cliff for her. We'd been practicing on the wall in the lodge all winter, but there was a big difference between plaster and the real thing. Audrey was doing terrifically well, but we'd been at it all morning and it was no wonder she was getting tired.

"We're almost there. Just a few more feet and it will all be worth it."

"It better be!" Audrey groaned, but her eyes were full of joy and exhilaration. She was an outdoors nut at heart, just like me.

"All right. You've made it! This is the top!" I helped pull Audrey up onto the flat surface of the precipice. At first she just lay there for a moment, resting her exhausted arms and legs. Then, she slowly got to her feet and took in the view, breathing in the crisp air deeply with satisfaction.

"You're right, this was definitely worth it," Audrey sighed. I put my arms around her and we enjoyed the breathtaking view together in silence for a few moments.

"Thank you for this," Audrey said. She wrapped her arms around my neck and kissed me lovingly on the lips. I held her tight and kissed her back, deepening the kiss.

"It's about to get even better," I grinned at her. "I've got a surprise for you."

"What is it?" Audrey looked around excitedly, expecting to find something hidden around the trees.

I reached into my pack and pulled out a small velvet box. Bending down on one knee, I held out the box to her.

"Audrey, these past six months have been the best days of my life. You've shown me a love and a happiness I never thought I could feel. I know things are moving quickly between us, but when you know you've found the person you want to be with the rest of your life, I don't see any reason to put things off. The one thing my past has taught me is that the future is never promised, so live today, love today, and do what you want to do today. Audrey Sawyer, I want to marry you and spend the rest of my life loving you. Will you please be my wife?"

I opened the box and showed her the glittering diamond ring inside. Audrey gasped and covered her face with her hands, crying tears of joy.

I let out a huge sigh of relief. I had been practicing that speech in my mind for weeks. I made Sean go with me to pick out the ring, and he had warned me I might be moving too fast, but I didn't see any reason to wait. Audrey was the perfect girl for me, and I wanted her to be my wife as soon as possible. The look of love and joy in her eyes told me I'd made the right decision. Now, all I needed was the official yes.

As I waited, my excitement turned to worry. Why hadn't she said yes yet?

I looked at Audrey and her eyes were running with tears. She dropped her hands from her face, and there was no smile on her lips. Just a grim frown.

"I'm sorry, Noah, but my answer is no," she sobbed softly.

I jumped to my feet. I felt like I'd been punched in the gut and kicked in the balls both at the same time. I wanted to be sick, but I was too pissed off to give her the satisfaction of seeing me break down like that.

"What do you mean?" I asked, feeling utterly humiliated. "You don't want to marry me?"

"I can't," she said.

I blinked at her. Suddenly, it all made sense. This had all been a game to her. I'd thought she was taking the past six months seriously, but she hadn't.

"I get it," I said.

"Noah, let me explain," Audrey cried.

"Explain what? How I'm good enough for a quick lay or to make you feel safe from the boogeyman at night, but not good enough to marry? How I'm not stable enough to build a future with or bring home to Mom and Dad? How I'm just a fucked-up ex-Marine living as a hermit in the woods?"

Audrey didn't disagree. Why would she? I'd spoken the truth that up till now she'd been too kind to say to my face. Well, now it was out there.

I grabbed the rope and rappelled down to the bottom. I saw her standing at the top and I yelled up to her, "Hurry up, if you don't want to walk the long way down."

When she reached the bottom, she held out her arms to hug me, but I turned my back on her. I didn't need her pity.

We drove in silence back to the cabin. The ring box was in my pocket, like a lead weight holding me down. Audrey got out of the truck and tried desperately to talk to me, but I couldn't bear to look at her, let alone listen to any of her bullshit.

"I'll stay at Sean's house tonight," I stated. "You have till the end of the weekend to clear your shit out of the cabin and find someplace else to live."

"Wait. Let's talk about all this," Audrey cried softly.

"What's there to talk about?" I growled. "I'm not the

kind of guy to just live with a girl forever and not marry her. If there's no future for us, why should we keep dragging things out? So unless you've changed your mind, I'd like you to be out by Sunday night. I don't want to have to see you again. It hurts too much."

As I drove away, I glanced in the rearview mirror and saw her collapsed in the road, sobbing. I wanted to turn around, pull her into my arms and hold her, but what good would it do? She had rejected me. What I thought we felt for each other was just a mirage, and so was this. It was best if I drove on and tried to put her behind me, even though I knew I would love her forever.

TWENTY-ONE

AUDREY

"**Y**ou can stay with me as long as you need," Elisa said, carrying a pile of my clothes into her spare bedroom and dropping them onto the bed.

"Thanks, but I don't want to be an imposition. I'll be out of here just as soon as I can find an apartment," I said gratefully.

"In North Haven, this time of year? Good luck!" Lauren said sarcastically as she came in carrying a box of my shoes, followed by Bethany with more clothes.

"Well, if not an apartment, maybe I can find a room for rent," I said with fake optimism, but it was clear I wasn't enthusiastic at the proposition. I never should have given up my cottage, but I'd been so happy staying at Noah's, I didn't consider what would happen when the fairy tale ended.

Elisa hugged me and said, "Don't even think about it. You've got a place to stay, right here with me. I'm glad my parents bought me this house, but I hate living in it alone. You'd be doing me a favor if you'd be my roommate."

I knew Elisa was just pandering to me, but I loved her for it. Hugging her back gratefully, I grinned and said,

"Well, what kind of friend would I be if I turned you down for a favor?"

Lauren stomped her foot and said, "Wait a minute! We can turn down favors? I don't have to be here helping you move all your crap from that cabin. Damn it! Why didn't anybody tell me?"

"I'll find a way to make it up to you," I said with a grin.

Lauren put her hands on her sassy hips and said, "Oh, I already know how you can do that. You are coming with me to Ladies' Night at the Tavern. Tonight is the night I'm getting that bartender to come home with me. You can serve as my wingwoman, distracting any interlopers who try to get in the way."

"No way," I said emphatically. "I just got out of a serious relationship. I won't be ready to date again for a long time."

"Are you kidding? Now is the perfect time to get back out there," Lauren coaxed, but I couldn't be swayed.

"Don't you realize I've had two marriage proposals from two different men in less than a year, both ending in really bad break-ups?" I sat on the bed feeling utterly cursed.

"Yeah, we're gonna need some details on that," Lauren said brashly.

Bethany was much more tactful. She sat on my left side and put her arm around my shoulders, while Elisa sat on my right, the two of them cocooning me in friendship.

Bethany said gently, "If you don't mind us asking, what did happen with you and Noah? You seemed so happy together."

"We were," I said, determined not to cry. "I guess maybe we were too happy. When Noah asked me to marry him, I was thrilled. I cried actual tears of joy, just like the girls I make fun of on TV. I was about to say yes when I realized it was just too fast. After all, we'd only been dating six months."

Lauren said, "Yeah, but you were living together that whole time, so that accelerates the process."

"No, it doesn't," I protested, but it seemed that Elisa and Bethany were on her side.

Elisa nodded and said, "You already knew each other's life habits, both the good and the bad. You knew what each other looked like in the morning before a shower and if the other snored at night. Living together six months is practically like being married already."

"Living together and making a lifetime commitment to each other under the eyes of God and the arm of the law are two completely different things," I stated, refusing to let my friends make light of the decision.

"All right. You've got a point." Elisa acquiesced. Then she gently asked, "So why did you live with him so long, after it was clear Wayne wasn't coming back?"

"I love him," I said firmly. "I liked living with Noah. He's so sweet and sensitive, but also so brave and strong. I liked waking up with his arms around me every morning and making love to him every night. He made me feel safe, happy, and in love. There's no one else I'd rather spend the rest of my life with."

"So, why not marry him then?" Bethany dared to ask, and the others nodded.

"I wanted to. I was about to say yes, when suddenly I thought of the last time I'd been proposed to. Wayne wasn't always a jerk. He started out a nice guy, charming and sweet, just like Noah. As I realized Noah and I hadn't really known each other that long, I began to worry about all the worst-case scenarios. What if Noah changed like Wayne had? What if he became jealous and possessive? What if he became controlling and forced me to change who I was? What if I lost myself again? I just couldn't risk going through that again. I already survived that emotional abuse and stalking once. I refuse to be victimized again. And honestly, the way Noah reacted to my saying no was over the top. It was just like I'd feared."

"I get it, Audrey," Elisa said.

My friends wrapped themselves around me in a group hug. I didn't even realize I had tears streaming down my face until Bethany handed me a tissue.

"I think you did the right thing in wanting to take things slower," Lauren said, "but I know it still hurts."

"Sorry," I apologized as I blew my nose noisily. I caught a glimpse of my reflection in the dresser mirror with my red, weepy eyes and groaned. "Ugh, I'm such a mess, literally and metaphorically."

"All right, enough of this wallowing," Lauren clapped her hands like she was addressing a classroom of kids. "Tonight is Ladies' Night. I say we all go to the Tavern to celebrate being four single women. The first round's on me!"

Bethany and Elisa both cheered and started freshening their lipstick and fluffing their hair. I just stepped back and shook my head. "You three go ahead. I'm not ready yet. Besides, it's been a long day."

"We can all stay in. Pop open some wine and watch old movies," Elisa suggested kindly, but it was clear the group was less than enthused.

"No, seriously. You girls go and have a good time. I could use some time to myself," I insisted.

After a bit more convincing, my friends all left and I was finally alone.

What had I done? I had alienated the first guy I'd truly

loved. I felt like an idiot. But when he'd proposed, a part of me froze. I just couldn't jump into an engagement so soon. And when I'd tried to explain, Noah wouldn't listen.

The spare room Elisa had given me was cute, with a four-poster bed and matching dresser. It was decorated in modern chic with brightly colored throw pillows on the bed and cheerful art on the walls. It was pretty, but I much preferred the gentler country beauty of Noah's cabin with his hand-carved chair and crocheted throw blanket.

As I started to unpack my things, I realized just how difficult a chore it was going to be. Everything reminded me of Noah. The leggings I wore the first time we met, the top I wore the first time we kissed, the perfume he gave me for my birthday, and the book he bought me just because it was written by my favorite author.

Soon tears were pouring down my cheeks again. Christ, I was going to dehydrate to death at this rate! I needed to get away from all the memories. I put on my favorite running clothes (ugh, more memories of Noah!) and decided to go for a run.

Running always cleared my head and made all my stresses seem more manageable. The rhythm of my feet on the ground soon matched the rhythm of my breathing and I began to unwind.

The land around Elisa's house was beautiful, with tall trees growing, the first budding leaves of spring, and daffodils just popping their yellow heads from the ground. Eventually, I slowed to a walk, enjoying the cool air as the late afternoon sun set below the horizon.

"Who are you?"

I looked up to see a little girl calling out to me as she walked along the top of the fence bordering her yard like it was a balance beam.

"I'm Audrey." I was taken aback by the precociously adorable little girl. I guessed her to be about six years old. She had reddish-brown pigtails that bobbed around her freckled cheeks.

"I'm Maisy! Are you my new neighbor?" she asked.

"No. I'm staying with a friend for a few days. She lives just down that way," I pointed in the direction I thought Elisa lived, but that was clearly wrong. Somehow I'd gotten turned around. I looked to the east, but that was wrong too. The west wasn't right either. Crap! When was I going to learn not to go running shortly after moving into a new place without at least taking my cell phone?

As I turned in a dizzying circle, the little girl said brightly, "If you're lost, always look for a police officer or a trusted adult to help you."

"Thanks, but there don't seem to be any police officers out here on this country road," I said. "How about a trusted adult? Are your parents home?"

"Never tell a stranger if your parents are home," the little girl said, and I had to stifle a laugh.

"I think you mean never tell a stranger if your parents are *not* home. It's okay to let them talk to your parents."

"Oh, yeah!" Maisy's face brightened. She ran across her yard towards an old barn, shouting out, "Daddy! A strange lady is lost and can't find her way home!"

Oh, God, could this get any more embarrassing?

Suddenly, a man emerged from the barn and started walking toward me. I wanted to faint. He was the perfect image of Noah, only he didn't have a beard and was a little bit older. He was tall, well over six feet, with Noah's same chiseled features and deep blue eyes, only his lacked that hardness that Noah's often had except in those moments when we were alone together and he finally let his guard down. Only now that I'd hurt him, I'd never see those blue eyes gazing at me tenderly again.

"Hi, my daughter tells me you need some help with directions." The man extended a friendly handshake. "I'm Owen Cole."

I should have known! This was Noah's brother. Noah had mentioned Owen to me before. The older brother had lost his first wife and was newly re-married. He was also a talented woodworker. He'd made the beautiful hand-carved chair in Noah's cabin I'd so often admired.

He gave me a smile and started happily explaining the road to me. "Folks get lost out here all the time. The main road actually veers off back at the tall oak, but if you keep going straight, it turns into a private road, which leads you here to my property. It looks like you jogged here, so if you want I'll give you a ride back to civilization."

"Listen, Owen, you don't know me, but I've been living with your brother for the past six months," I said, swallowing back the lump that had grown in my throat.

"What?" Owen stared at me in shock. "Jared has a girlfriend living with him?"

"No, not that brother. I've been living with Noah," I explained.

"Noah?" Owen looked like he needed to sit down. He glanced down at his daughter and said, "Maisy, go into the house and play."

"Okay, Daddy!" She skipped off happily, leaving the two of us to stare at each other awkwardly over the fence.

"How is he? Is everything okay?" The way Owen shoved his hands in his pockets reminded me of Noah when he was uncomfortable.

"Everything is fine. Actually, it's not. Noah and I just broke up. He proposed to me, and I didn't say yes."

"Oh, boy." Owen looked down at his boots. The air between us was so heavy, it was suffocating.

"Yeah," I drew in a deep breath. "So, I have a feeling he could use some family support right now. Only I know he won't ask for it. I didn't intend to tell you this, but since I got lost on your road and met your daughter by accident, it kinda feels like fate. Like maybe this is my chance to do something good for him after breaking his heart."

"Listen, I appreciate what you're trying to do here, but Noah's made it clear he doesn't want me or any of his brothers going out to his cabin to bother him."

"I know he's been that way for a long time, but he's changed recently. He told me himself that he's been alienated from his brothers long enough. I think he's ready to make amends, and my refusing his proposal might just be the opening he needs to lean on his brothers for support."

Owen just kept staring at his boots, not saying anything. Finally he looked at me and said, "Do you need a ride home or not?"

"Yes, thank you," I replied, feeling disappointed but not surprised. After everything Noah had told me about the way he'd treated his brothers, I couldn't really blame him. I just wished he could see how much Noah had changed.

"I'll get my truck," Owen said. We drove in silence as he took me back to Elisa's home address.

As I got out of the truck, I said, "Thanks for the ride. And Owen, you brothers are the only family Noah has left. Maybe it's time you all gave him one more chance."

"He really said he wants to make amends?" Owen asked, and I nodded tearfully. Owen was quiet for a long time, then he said, "All right, maybe I'll stop by and check on him."

"Thank you," I whispered and watched him drive away.

It hurt to see someone looking so much like Noah, and made me miss him all the more, but maybe this was what fate intended for me all along. I couldn't be his bride, but I could mend the hole in his heart by reuniting him with his brothers.

I walked back into Elisa's house, not even noticing the car that drove slowly past, or the driver that snapped my picture as he went by.

I'd been protected for so long, I'd lost my edge. It was too bad that protection was now gone.

The cabin was empty. She was fucking gone.

Somehow I'd expected that when I came home Sunday night, she'd still be there, telling me she'd made a mistake and that of course she wanted to marry me.

It was a ridiculous fantasy, and I shouldn't have been surprised that she'd actually moved out, but the reality of it was still like a punch to the balls.

I slept in a sleeping bag on the floor that night because I couldn't stand lying in our bed without her. I did the same thing the next night and the night after that.

By Wednesday, my back was fucking killing me and I moved back to the bed, but I was up most of the night tossing and turning.

It was unfortunate for Sean that he ran into me Thursday morning, a little before noon.

"Hey, there you are," Sean greeted me with his usual cheerfulness. "I was wondering if you planned on coming to work at the lodge any time soon?"

"No," I said. I was deep in the middle of a project and I didn't have time to take spoiled tourists from the city out sightseeing in the forest. They could find deer and avoid getting poison oak all on their own for all I cared.

"With the weather getting warmer, we're getting busier," Sean said tentatively. "I could use a hand."

"Well, then hire one. We've got the budget for it now," I snapped. "I've got to clear these trees. There needs to be a fence here to separate my cabin from the lodge. I don't want fucking hikers getting lost on the trail and wandering onto my property."

The scenario reminded me too much of how I met Audrey, and I just couldn't stand going through that kind of heartbreak again.

"So, you're clearing all the trees by hand to build a fence?" Sean sounded dumbfounded, but I had no idea why. It made perfect fucking sense to me.

I swung my ax, feeling the blade bite into the wood with a solid, gratifying thunk. Several more good thwacks and it fell to the ground with a heavy thud, vibrating the ground and making Sean jump back several feet.

He stared as I grabbed the felled tree by one of its sturdier branches and dragged it single-handedly next to the others. Later, I'd cut them all down into logs for firewood and stack them by the cabin.

"So, I can see you're too busy to come to the lodge," Sean stammered nervously, "but I thought you should know there are some people here asking to see you."

"Tell them I'm not available. If they don't like it, they can fuck off," I barked.

"It's a little late for that," Sean said, indicating the path behind me. I turned and looked, and saw four large figures walking towards me.

It was my brothers!

Ethan, Owen, Gavin, and even my little brother, Jared.

They'd all come! I couldn't believe it. For a moment, my heart soared. God, it was so fucking good to see them all again.

"What the hell are you guys doing here?" I asked, sounding a lot angrier than I meant to.

"We came to see if you needed a hand with anything," Owen said simply.

"And it's a good thing we did, 'cause it looks like you do," Gavin gave me a brotherly slap on the back that earned him one of my best glares.

"It looks like we're clearing these trees, so let's get to work, guys," Ethan called out. He was the oldest and always liked telling everyone what to do. No wonder he'd become a doctor.

They opened up huge gear bags, and my brothers all produced work gloves, hatchets, and axes. Owen had a chainsaw.

I pointed at Sean and said, "Did you do this?"

"They all just showed up at the lodge this morning wanting to see you," Sean shrugged. "I had a feeling you wouldn't come down until you were done with whatever this is, so they offered to help."

"If I need help, I'll ask for it," I growled. I hated to be thought of as weak. Somehow my brothers must have found out about my break-up with Audrey. In a small town full of nothing but gossips, it was no big surprise. Well, I didn't want their pity. It was too humiliating.

"That's the thing about family," Ethan said. "You don't always need to ask for their help. Sometimes they just give it to you anyway."

I glared at Sean the traitor as he walked away, leaving me alone with my brothers. Fine, they could help if they wanted to, but that didn't mean I had to like it.

I kept my mouth shut tight, refusing to say a word as my brothers worked alongside me, felling the trees I had marked and cutting them down into logs. Soon, we had a regular assembly line going, and the woodpile started stacking up quickly.

I had to admit, it felt good to have my family by my side, not judging me, not pressuring me, not trying to give me unwanted advice. They were just there, the five of us Cole brothers, doing what had to be done. There was something deeply satisfying in that.

By late afternoon, we had completed a job that would have taken me a week on my own. Looking at all we'd accomplished together, I forgot that I was mad at them, and all I felt was pride.

"Thanks, guys. It's beer-thirty," I said. They followed me down to the lodge, where the chef served us up giant sandwiches piled high with meat and vegetables, and ice-cold bottles of beer.

As they stuffed their faces, my brothers chatted with each other, sharing inside jokes and giving each other a hard time. It made me feel jealous and more than a little left out.

"So what are you guys really doing out here?" I damn well knew there had to be a reason they all spontaneously showed up.

"We figured it had been long enough since we spent time together, all five of us," Owen said, and the others nodded.

"That's it? No bullshit?" I sounded like I was interrogating enemy combatants, but they were my brothers, and somehow I believed them.

"That's it," Gavin insisted. "You're our brother and we all miss you. You don't want to talk to us, that's fine. You don't have to. It's good enough just to be around you."

"But if you ever do want to talk about anything, we're here for you." Ethan put his hand on my shoulder, and without meaning to, I broke down and started yapping.

I told them everything about Audrey, and how happy she'd made me these past six months, and how I didn't know how to go on without her.

Owen reminded me that he'd felt the same way when his wife died of cancer, and I suddenly felt like a complete shithead. One of my brothers had suffered a real tragedy, while all that had happened to me was I got dumped by a woman I shouldn't have fallen in love with in the first place.

I knew from the start that I should have stayed away from Audrey Sawyer. After all, everybody I ever cared for was taken from me. First my parents, then my platoon. At least Audrey hadn't died, but our relationship had, which was still a kind of death.

My brothers offered me all sorts of advice. Some said to forget her and move on. Others said to fight for her. Gavin thought I should be patient while Jared thought I should keep playing the field. I listened and laughed along, but I already knew exactly what I had to do.

It was time I faced the truth. I was cursed, and the best thing I could do was to keep my heart closed tight and never let anyone in again.

My brothers' appearance had shown me that we shared a bond that I'd been sorely missing in my life. We were the Cole brothers, and that was a relationship no earthly force could sever.

But I knew I couldn't let even them get too close, or I'd risk their lives as well.

"Thanks for coming out today, guys. I'm sorry I was such an asshole these past few years," I said, raising my beer bottle in a toast.

"Only the past few years? You've been an asshole since we were kids!" Ethan teased, and we all started laughing and roughhousing again.

God, it felt good to be around family again. I hadn't realized how much I missed that camaraderie until they showed up.

That night, I walked to my cabin with my spirits lifted. But as soon as I walked in the door and saw how empty it was, my heart sank.

There was only one thing missing in my life, and it was the biggest: Audrey's love.

I had some good things going—my business was picking up, and my brothers cared enough to show up out of the blue. But none of that mattered without Audrey to share it all with.

But that was something I would simply have to learn to live without. That was for everyone else in the world to enjoy, but not for me. Living the rest of my life alone, with my heart closed off to love, never having a woman to hold and share my joys with—well, that was my curse, and I just had to accept it.

TWENTY-THREE
AUDREY

"You have to do it for me," I insisted.

"But I have plans this weekend, and they don't involve wrecking my nails out in the wilderness or babysitting a bunch of thirteen-year-olds. I deal with those same kids all during the week. Saturday is supposed to be my day to get away from it all and relax."

"I know, but I can't go. He'll be there, and I'm just not ready to face him after everything that's happened between us." I clutched onto Elisa's nightshirt, and reduced myself to begging pitifully. "Please. You're my best friend."

"Okay, fine. I'll supervise the Explorers' outing in your place, but you owe me big." Elisa glared, even as I hugged her tight.

"Thank you! Thank you! Thank you!" I squealed, barely containing the urge to jump up and down like a child on Christmas.

"Enough. One of these days I'll be the one needing to avoid an incredibly rich, handsome, sexy... wait a minute, why exactly did you break up with him again?"

"Ha-ha," I laughed without humor. "You'd better hurry up. The kids will be arriving at the lodge soon."

I helped Elisa get dressed, packed her sunscreen in her backpack, and shoved her out the door.

"Have a great time!" I waved cheerily, but Elisa just flipped me off as she drove away.

I should have felt relieved that she had agreed to go in my place, but I didn't. No doubt the kids would wonder why I wasn't there, but what about Noah? Would he miss me too or would he be glad I wasn't there? The disappointing notion that he wouldn't even miss me kept haunting my thoughts, and made it impossible for me not to think about him.

I'd had break-ups before, but none had ever made me feel so miserable. I missed Noah every minute of every day. I couldn't stop wondering what he was doing, how he was feeling, and if I'd made a huge mistake turning down his proposal. After all, we had been so incredibly happy together, until I blew it by turning him down. The wonderful months I'd spent living with Noah had been nothing like the stress I'd suffered while living with Wayne.

Noah was sensitive, caring, brave, strong, and sweetly protective. Not to mention sexy as hell. No one had ever made me feel the incredible pleasures he gave me when we made love in our cozy cabin in the woods, or under the trees in a soft bed of leaves in the forest, or in the tall grasses of the meadow where the deer grazed. Noah made me see the forest in a whole new way, and we couldn't get enough of each other or being out in the woods.

Noah had a love for nature that was contagious. I loved going hiking and camping with him, and just seeing the passion and joy he felt for the forest. His genuine love for nature shone through in everything he did, which was probably the main reason his business was thriving so much. In fact, I'd heard a rumor that his competitor, Paul Hathaway, had to shut down his business because Noah was so good at what he did. I wished I could have seen the look on Noah's face when he heard the news that his biggest rival had been defeated, but of course I'd never get to share his joys or his struggles again.

I felt selfish for refusing to marry him just because my own hardships had made me afraid. Noah had been through a lot worse in his life, and he wasn't shrinking away from love. He was running straight towards it, fearlessly embracing the challenges of marriage despite all the heartbreak he'd suffered. What was I doing? I was running away, refusing to marry the one man I truly loved just because I'd had a bad experience with an ex-boyfriend.

My heart had been shattered into a million pieces. And I had only myself to blame. I'd screwed up the best relationship of my life by not accepting Noah's proposal. If only he would have let me explain!

And to make matters worse, Wayne had reared his ugly head again.

The past few days, he'd started emailing me once more, demanding that I marry him and go live with him in North Carolina again. Each email he sent made me feel more afraid and helpless. He also demanded to know where I was. It gave me some comfort that he apparently wasn't sure of my location, but at night I recalled with terror the time he'd shown up at the middle school searching for me. The way his voice had boomed through the halls... it still made me shiver. Elisa had thrown him off my trail that time, but what was to stop him from turning up in North Haven again?

I shuddered as I remembered the last email he'd sent. I

kept them all because they could be used as evidence in any kind of legal action I might pursue, but I hated reading them.

Soon you'll be my wife, Audrey. You'll see. We'll be perfect together. You'll come back to live with me in Charlotte, and we'll be a happy family again.

Take a few days to consider my proposal. I'll want to know your answer soon, and it better be yes.

Then you'll just have to tell me where you are, and I'll come get you. But even if you don't tell me, I'll find you. Don't you worry about that.

As long as Wayne was looking for me, I'd never feel safe.

I heaved a great sigh. I needed to go for a run to clear my head.

I put on my running shoes – grabbing my cell phone this time – and stepped out the front door.

Just as I locked the door and bounded off the front step, my phone rang. It was a number I didn't recognize, but a local one, so I swiped at the screen to take the call.

"Hello?" I answered.

Silence. Then, faintly, breathing.

Fear closed around me.

"Hello?" I repeated.

But there was no response. Just the steady sound of someone breathing. *Waiting.*

I swallowed a lump in my throat. I hated being afraid like this.

"Wayne? Is that you?" I whispered, my voice wavering.

Then, they hung up. The line was dead.

Standing in Elisa's front yard, I looked around. An eerie feeling crept over me. Everything looked the same – the neighboring houses, the empty streets – but I suddenly felt uneasy, as if safe, homey little North Haven had just taken a sinister turn.

I went inside the house and locked the door.

I'm sure it's nothing. One of my students just got my number and is playing a prank.

But as I moved through the house, lowering all the blinds with trembling hands, I couldn't shake the feeling that I was terribly wrong.

"All right, Explorers, as soon as everyone gets here, we'll begin," I announced.

The lodge was full of excited young faces, eager to learn how to rock climb, but for the third week in a row, Audrey hadn't shown, sending her friend Elisa in her place yet again. I kept holding onto the hope that we could at least resume a casual level of friendship for the sake of the Explorers. It wasn't much, but at least it would be a way I could still see her beautiful face.

Elisa walked up to me, and said quietly, "Everyone is here. Audrey has permanently resigned from the Explorers."

"I see," I said curtly. So that was it. Audrey couldn't even stand to be in the same room with me for the sake of the kids. It was truly over between us.

I'd been carefully planning what I'd say when I finally got to see her again, even practicing my speech in the mirror like a damn fool. I had acted like a fucking idiot when I broke up with her just because she wouldn't marry me. At the very least, I should have let her explain her reasons.

Now Audrey refused to even answer when I called, and there was too much to say for me to try and text. So, I thought I was playing it smart by giving her some space. I thought maybe then she would see that we could at least work together as friends helping the Explorers, but I should have fucking known better. Of course she wouldn't be here today, especially after the way I treated her, in what should have been the most romantic moment of our lives. I was a fucking idiot, and I'd lost the woman I loved because of my own stupidity, not because of some curse.

"Mr. Cole, are we really going to climb that?" a student asked, pulling me from my thoughts. She was looking up at the rock wall that extended from the floor of the lodge all the way to the top of the vaulted ceiling.

Grinning down at her, I said, "Yes we are, but don't worry. You'll be perfectly safe the entire time, thanks to ropes and harnesses. I promise, you won't fall, even if you completely let go of the rock wall. Who wants to volunteer to demonstrate?"

A dozen hands flew up in the air, and for the next several hours I was too busy to think about Audrey and how much I missed her.

When the lunch break came, I made a point of sitting next to Elisa while the kids attacked the chef's specialty pizza like a pack of starving hyenas.

"I brought you a slice, so you don't have to risk your life trying to get one," I said, handing her a paper plate and a napkin.

"Thanks. Audrey said you were brave," Elisa teased, but then it was clear she regretting saying Audrey's name in front of me and quickly started shoving food into her mouth.

"Is she doing okay?" I asked softly.

"Yeah," Elisa said uncomfortably, unsure if she should be talking to her best friend's ex-boyfriend about her. "Audrey's been staying with me until she finds a new place, but..."

There was clearly something bothering Elisa, but she was conflicted about telling me. I needed to reassure her it was okay.

"What? Just tell me!" I said urgently, making Elisa jump.

Fuck! I didn't mean to scare the shit out of her.

Way to go, dumbass.

Shaking my head, I said, "I'm sorry. I worry about her and I miss her. It's been hard not knowing if she's safe, if she's comfortable, if she's happy. I didn't mean to act like an asshole."

Elisa smiled. "You really do love her, don't you?"

"I do," I said, and I was surprised by just how much.

Elisa leaned close to my ear and spoke in a low voice so no one could hear.

"She would kill me for telling you this, but Audrey's not okay. Her ex, Wayne, has been harassing her, sending her scary emails. The police told us there's nothing they can do unless he shows up in town. I don't think he knows where she is, but I can tell she's still really frightened by him."

"That son of a bitch!" I muttered under my breath. My blood was raging, and I had to force my fists to unclench. "I'll make sure he never scares her again. I have to go to her now!"

"Aren't you forgetting the little matter of all these kids?" Elisa pointed out, and I was suddenly reminded that I was responsible for a lodge full of young teenagers until their parents came to get them. "Let's just finish today's lesson. They'll all get picked up in just two hours and then you can go to her," Elisa said. "She's safe at my place for now."

I knew she was right, but I hated knowing Audrey was vulnerable and scared while I was up here playing rock climber. If something happened to her during this time, I'd never forgive myself.

"I just need a moment to compose myself," I said and stalked off behind the practice wall to try and calm my mind. Deep breaths in a quiet corner. It was a calming technique that had served me well, but not today.

"Mr. Cole!" a young male voice called out, startling the hell out of me. It was fucking Tyler Hathaway, and I'd nearly tripped over him.

"What are you doing back here, kneeling on the floor?" I cried out.

"Nothing, I got lost," Tyler stammered, hiding his hands behind his back. Shit, the kid was a bad fucking liar.

"What the hell is this?" I yanked his hands forward and snatched what he was holding. My climbing rope and a knife. He'd been fraying the rope, trying to weaken it. The little vandal was too dumb to know that I checked my rope thoroughly before each climb, so the trick never would have worked, but he obviously didn't know that.

The realization that he'd been intentionally trying to hurt me pissed me off. I glared deep into his eyes and growled low, "Are you the one who's been vandalizing my property all year long, cutting little holes in things, damaging supplies, slicing cords?"

"No. It wasn't me!" Tyler cried, visibly shaking. All I had to do was arch my left brow at him, and he fucking broke like a toothpick.

"Okay, it was me," Tyler cried out. "I was trying to help my father. His business started struggling the minute yours opened. First I called Save the Salamanders. I thought they could shut you down, but when they couldn't, I knew it was up to me. I thought if I could do enough damage, it would ruin your reputation, and customers would come back to my father."

I felt sorry for the kid. I knew what it was like to have a father's business mean the world to you. You'd do anything in hopes that maybe you could earn an ounce of his love, or maybe just some of his attention. I knew I should be pissed off at the kid, but I just felt sorry for him.

I gestured for Tyler to leave, and he ran off. As much as I empathized with him, I had an obligation to tell Elisa, and she was utterly mortified.

"I'll turn in a report the moment I get back to the school, and he'll be suspended immediately," Elisa promised, but that didn't feel like justice to me.

"Let me drive the kid home. I'll talk to his father and we'll see if we can work out a way to punish Tyler without pulling him out of school," I suggested.

"Are you sure?" Elisa asked as she called Tyler over to us. The poor kid looked like he was going to the executioner as he walked slowly towards us.

Looking at his mournful face, I nodded my head. "I'm sure. Come on, Tyler, let's get you home."

The kid was dead silent as I drove him home. When his father answered the door, he was shocked to see me standing there with his son, but Paul's expression quickly turned to one of suspicion.

"What the hell are you doing here, Noah?" Paul grabbed his son away from me and protectively drew him to his side.

"I think you'll want to sit down for what I have to say," I warned him. "May I come in?"

"Fine," Paul said hesitantly. Balancing awkwardly on the edge of his sofa, I told Paul everything about what Tyler had been doing, and why.

"So, you're here to tell me you're going to press charges?" Paul was on his feet, his face red and contorted with anger. "Or you plan to sue me for everything I've got? Well, you won't get much! I've been losing money since the day you opened Pine Creek Lodge. I put a second mortgage on the house, and now we'll probably lose our home. After dedicating my entire life to nature preservation and protecting the habitat of the Shenandoah salamander, it looks like I'm the one who's endangered now. I'm at rock bottom, and you're here to see it."

Paul looked completely broken. The man had been my competitor and rival for as long as I could remember, but he was a good man and he deserved a better fate. I'd just never considered how my success might be affecting others like him, and perhaps I should have.

"Actually, I'm here to offer you a job," I said as the idea took shape in my mind.

Paul took a step back and blinked. "What? If you think I'm going to work for you in some pity position, you can think again. I've got unique skills that someone will pay good money for."

"I know you do. This isn't a pity offer. I've been thinking long and hard about creating a program dedicated to educating the public about the Shenandoah salamander, while preserving and protecting its habitat. I'd need someone very knowledgeable to head up the program. What do you say? Would you be interested in the position?"

Paul's eyes lit up, and so did Tyler's.

"Say yes, Dad! I can't wait to tell everyone in school my dad is in charge of a program protecting the salamanders! You'll be a real hero!"

Paul smiled weakly. "Not quite, son, but I would like to discuss the details of the job."

"Terrific," I grinned and took his hand. I think it was the first time Paul and I had ever officially shaken hands. "Let's meet at the lodge in a few days and we can work out the details."

"I'd like that." Paul had tears of emotion brimming in his eyes, so I graciously left before they spilled over. The moment the door to Paul's house closed behind me, I heard Tyler whooping with joy, and it put a grin on my face.

It felt really gratifying to have done something good, not just for the lodge and the salamander, but on a much more personal level. Today, I'd helped a local family.

I'd spent my life despising Paul Hathaway, but he was just a husband with a wife and son, trying his best to pay his bills while holding down a business dedicated to nature. Then I'd swooped in with my money and my prebuilt luxury lodge and stolen his dreams away. No wonder his son resented me.

But today I'd turned all that around. I'd taken down the wall between us and used it to build a bridge. It was one of the most rewarding experiences of my life. I just wished Audrey was there with me to share the moment. Nothing meant nearly as much to me anymore if I couldn't share it with her.

But at the moment, Audrey was probably terrified out of her mind at Elisa's. I jumped in my truck and pressed my foot down on the accelerator, all the way to the floor. I didn't want her to spend another moment in fear of Wayne – or thinking I didn't care about her.

She needed to know I would be there to protect her from any danger, including her ex, and that it didn't matter if she was willing to marry me or not. I just wanted to have her in my life.

I had to get to Audrey as fast as I could.

"How did it go?" I asked Elisa the moment she walked through the door after taking the Explorers rock climbing. Taking on that club may have started out as an obligation, but it had turned into one of my greatest joys, and I truly missed it now.

"Fine," Elisa said evasively. Usually she couldn't stop talking, so I knew something was up.

"What are you not telling me?" I insisted on knowing.

"Don't be mad, but I told him."

"You told who what?"

Elisa cringed. "I told Noah everything about Wayne harassing you, and how you were scared."

"What? How could you?" I cried out angrily. I'd been betrayed by my best friend.

"He asked about you. I could tell he was really worried about you. He loves you."

"Yeah, well, he's got a funny way of showing it," I pouted.

"Oh, you mean by asking you to marry him and being heartbroken when you said no? Yeah, that is an odd way for a man to show a woman he loves her." Elisa's voice was dripping with sarcasm.

"Elisa, Wayne's threats and stalking have been awful. You don't know what it's like to be pressured into marrying someone you don't love, and who's a psycho," I snapped. "There's nothing worse. It eats away at you inside until you're just a shell of who you used to be."

"Is that how you feel with Noah, or are you projecting your problems with Wayne onto this relationship? Don't let that jerk ruin the best relationship you've ever had."

"Why are you so damn sensible?" I complained a moment before I hugged her. Resting my head on her shoulder, I said, "Maybe you're right. But it's too late. I already broke Noah's heart. He's never going to want to be with me. And while you were gone..."

I started to mention the creepy phone call I'd gotten earlier, but I cut myself off. I didn't want to worry Elisa any more than she already was. The woman was giving me a house to live in until I found my own place, and I didn't want to burden her with any more of my problems. Besides, the phone call was probably nothing.

"What?" Elisa asked.

I shook my head. "Nothing. I just miss Noah. And I blew it with him."

Elisa stroked my hair away from my forehead and said, "You know, I don't think it's too late to patch things up with him. I saw the look in that man's eyes, and he is still in love with you. In fact, he's coming here soon to talk to you."

"Are you serious?" I flew across the room to look in the mirror. "Oh, God! I'm a mess! Hand me a hairbrush and some mascara. No, lip gloss first, and I need to change clothes. I look like a homeless person."

Elisa helped me get ready for Noah, then looked at her

watch and said, "I'd better go. He just had to take Tyler home and then he was coming right over. He should be here any minute, and I don't want to be in the way. I'll be at Lauren's. Good luck!"

Elisa winked lasciviously, and I laughed and hurled a throw pillow at her from the couch. It hit the door just as she closed it, and fell to the floor.

I felt nervous as I fluffed the pillow before placing it back on the couch. I imagined Noah sitting on the couch and me beside him, and I quickly rearranged the pillows, then arranged them yet again. The more I thought about what I would say to Noah, the more anxious I became.

What if he couldn't forgive me for breaking his heart? What if he didn't love me anymore?

I heard a truck rumble to a stop outside, and my heart jumped in my chest. It must be Noah! He was here!

Eagerly, I rushed to the door and without even waiting for him to knock, I threw open the door only to come face to face with the wrong man.

I'd run right into my worst nightmare.

Wayne towered over me, a demented smile playing on his lips.

"Hello, Audrey. It's been a long time. I thought maybe you forgot about me."

His voice made me freeze, paralyzed by fear.

A scream rose up in me, but before it could leave my lungs, he clamped his meaty hand over my open mouth.

He grabbed my arm and shoved his way inside before I could even think to slam the door in his face, forcing me to walk backwards as he did so.

Wayne shoved me back onto the couch, and I sat down hard, rubbing my arm where he'd left a mark.

As he shut the door behind him and turned the lock, he whistled.

"My, my. Don't you look lovely this evening." Wayne looked down at me with a disgusting leer, and I suddenly wanted to cover myself. "You're all dressed up for the occasion."

Wayne looked around Elisa's house appraisingly, taking it all in. I watched him with fear and disgust. Who knew how long he'd been watching me – maybe ever since that day at the middle school. He had been lying in his emails about not knowing where I was.

"This is a nice place. You live here with someone?"

"I do." I lifted my chin defiantly. "My roommate will be home any minute. You'd better get out of here before then."

"The schoolteacher with the red curls?" Wayne chuckled cruelly. "I don't think so. She just left. Maybe she's running off again to meet that ex-boyfriend of yours, the hermit lumberjack."

"Noah's a wilderness guide," I said, feeling defensive of Noah despite my fear.

"Well, he's history now," Wayne said with a dangerous glint in his brooding eyes. "I've come to bring you back home with me, where you belong."

"No, Wayne. I already told you a long time ago, we aren't right for each other. You should move on and find someone who can truly make you happy."

"I've thought a lot about what you said these past months," Wayne said.

He pulled a large knife out of the sheath on his belt, and started using the blade to clean underneath his fingernails. Nausea rose inside me as I watched his erratic movements. The threat in his tone belied the sweetness of his words.

"Well, guess what?" he continued. "I've changed. I'm

ready to be the man you need. All you have to do is say you'll be my wife, and I'll be the man you've always wanted."

The tension in the air pressed in all around me, making it hard for me to breathe. The light reflected blindingly on his blade for a moment. The look in his eyes was so intense, it bore into me like a searing needle.

"I'm glad you've changed," I said carefully as I moved off the couch. I walked slowly across the room, inching my way toward the cordless phone on the kitchen counter. "But how can you say you want to marry me when you don't even know who the real me truly is?"

"Oh, I know the real you," Wayne said. With every step I took away from him, he took two towards me, closing the gap between us. "I've been watching you for months, going through your garbage, following you to the store and monitoring your every move. I know everything there is to know about you, and I'll be the perfect husband for you."

"No, Wayne," I said firmly, trying to keep the fear out of my voice. "I won't marry you. We're completely wrong for each other. In fact, I never want to see you again. Please leave and never come back."

"Oh, I'm leaving, only you're coming with me. We're going back home to North Carolina together, where I'm never letting you out of my sight again." His eyes darted toward the phone, and he returned the knife to its sheath.

"No, Wayne." I kept my voice strong and even. Despite my shaking hands and pounding heart, I wasn't going to let him bully me any longer. I refused to live in fear another day.

I lunged for the phone, but his own sudden movement made me freeze.

"Maybe this will change your mind."

Wayne pulled a handgun from his waistband. He held his arm out and pointed the weapon right at me.

Oh, God. This is it.

My heart froze in my chest, and I couldn't move. I just stared at that barrel pointing at my chest.

"Now pack your shit and let's go," he said with a sneer.

He forced me into the spare bedroom. I stood gawking at the gun, unblinking, until he barked at me to start packing. With trembling hands, I opened the dresser drawers. I could hardly think straight, but I grabbed the first thing I saw. In my panic, I dropped a stack of T-shirts on the floor.

"Hurry up!" he screamed at me.

I nodded and scrambled to gather the clothes. Tears flooded my eyes and blurred my vision. I knew if I rode off with Wayne, I might not survive. How was I going to get out of this?

Suddenly, I heard the sound of another truck parking outside. I held my breath in hopeful anticipation.

Maybe Noah's here.

When I caught a glance of Noah through the window as he passed by, my heart pounded ever more quickly. Hope was quickly replaced with new terror.

Wayne was acting crazy, and I was fearful for Noah's life. Wayne wouldn't think twice about shooting him. A sick feeling twisted my stomach as tears rolled down my cheeks.

Noah knocked on the front door, and Wayne grabbed me roughly by the arm and pulled me to him.

"Who the hell is that?" Wayne snapped.

"It's Noah Cole."

"Your ex-boyfriend? Maybe I should shoot him in the fucking head for interfering with our relationship."

"No. That will just bring the cops. I'll tell him to go

away," I said, my voice shaky. If Noah died because of me, I'd never be able to forgive myself.

I walked to the front door with Wayne right behind me.

"Don't even think about trying anything," Wayne whispered. I nodded and wiped the tears from my face.

Leaving the chain on the door, I opened it just a crack and peered out at Noah. I could feel Wayne's gun digging into my back.

"Noah, hi. This isn't a good time," I said brusquely.

"I came to talk to you, but I see you have company. Who's here?" He tried to peer into the house.

"No one. Elisa got a new truck. I just can't talk right now. Girls' night, you know. I'll call you later."

"Is everything all right?" Noah could tell something was wrong. Of course he could. I was a terrible liar and my voice sounded weird, even to me.

"Actually, everything's not all right. Elisa's going through an awful time right now and she really needs me. So if you could please leave, I'll talk to you later."

"Okay, fine." Noah nodded and turned to leave.

I breathed a sigh of relief that Noah wouldn't be harmed, even while fear for my own life mounted. I closed the door and turned to face my tormentor.

Wayne's cold eyes locked on mine for a split second, sending a chill through my core. I knew I'd have to leave with him soon.

Then, suddenly, Noah burst through the front door, breaking the chain and ripping the door off its hinges.

I screamed as Wayne quickly wrapped his arm around my throat and pulled me in front of him like a human shield. Noah lowered his stance, looking like an NFL linebacker ready for the tackle. I could feel Wayne's pulse racing as he held me hostage.

"Let her go," Noah commanded forcefully.

"No. She's my wife! She's going to marry me and if she doesn't, I'll blow her brains out!" Wayne said, dragging me along with him as he slowly backed up toward the door.

"Are you kidding?" Noah scoffed, advancing cautiously towards us step by step. "Audrey Sawyer is the most independent woman I know. She's like a force of nature that can't be contained. You can't force her into marriage, and if you did, she would lose that fire that makes her so amazing. It would need to be her choice, not your demand."

"Shut up!" Wayne shouted. "We're leaving. And then we're getting married!"

"Good luck with that," Noah said sarcastically. "My truck is parked behind yours. Looks like you're trapped in the driveway. Why don't you put down the gun and just walk away before anybody gets hurt?"

Wayne glanced out the window and saw that Noah was telling the truth. I heard him swear under his breath as Noah carefully inched closer, shrinking the distance between them.

My heart was pounding so hard, I could hear the rush of blood in my veins. I knew Noah would do whatever he had to do to protect me, even if meant sacrificing his own life. But I wasn't afraid for my own safety, it was Noah I was worried about. I couldn't let him die for me. If anyone deserved to make it out of this situation alive, it was Noah, not me, and I was determined to make sure he did.

Wayne dug his gun into my temple so hard it made me cry out. Shouting at Noah, he said, "Give me the keys to your truck! Drop them on the floor and put your hands in the air! Do it, or her blood will be a stain on your soul forever!"

Noah had a strange look on his face for just a moment.

Then he locked eyes with me, as if letting me know everything would be okay. I watched in fear as Noah slowly set his keys on the floor, then raised his hands in the air in the surrender position.

Wayne took the gun from my temple and, to my horror, aimed it straight at Noah.

Time stood still as I watched the awful scene.

I knew in that moment he was going to shoot the man I loved. I couldn't let him. I had to do something.

Instinctively, I kicked back, striking him in the knee with my heel as hard as I could. In that same moment, I thrust back with my elbow, striking him right in the gut. Wayne cried out in surprise as he doubled over in pain.

"Audrey, get down!" Noah shouted as he leapt forward. I dove to the side as he tackled Wayne to the floor. The gun was knocked loose from his grip and skittered across the floor.

I went to pick it up, and in that moment the police came streaming through the front door.

I held my breath as they rushed toward Wayne. Three officers surrounded him as Noah held him in place. The police handcuffed Wayne and pulled him to his feet as he kicked and fought, his face turning bright red. One officer retrieved Wayne's gun.

Noah stood at the ready, watching Wayne like a hawk.

Seeing that awful, violent man cuffed, I could finally breathe again. Wayne hurled a string of obscenities at me and Noah, but his words hardly registered in my mind.

All I could think was, *I'm safe now. Noah's here.*

Elisa slipped in the front door and ran to me.

"Thank goodness you're safe," Elisa breathed, wrapping an arm around me. "I came back for my sweater. When I saw that truck in the driveway, I knew you were in trouble and called the police."

"Thank God you did," I said, grateful for my best friend.

The officers finally dragged Wayne away, leaving the house suddenly still and quiet.

Across the room, Noah turned to look at me.

I locked eyes with Audrey, and we ran to each other. I never wanted to be apart from her again.

"Are you all right? Did he hurt you?" I checked Audrey for injuries before pulling her into my arms and holding her tight.

She was shaking against me as I held her. "I'm fine," she said. "I'm just glad you're okay."

Elisa stepped outside to talk to the police, and I pulled Audrey to the couch.

When she was in my arms, her shock seemed to wear off. I knew that feeling well – reality hitting you like a ton of bricks.

She broke down in tears. I held her for a long time as she wept quietly, her shoulders shaking.

"Everything's going to be okay," I murmured, soothing her as I held her tightly.

After some time, her cries died down, and she finally looked up at me with her tear-stained face.

"You're all right now. You're safe," I said. I grabbed her

bottle of water from the coffee table and handed it to her. She took a long drink, then turned her gaze to me.

"I can believe that now that you're here," she said. "I was so scared, Noah."

"He's gone now," I said. "He can't hurt you."

"Thanks to you," she said. "I don't know what I would have done if you hadn't shown up."

I didn't want to think about that. I was just glad I'd arrived when I did.

Taking deep breaths, she looked around the living room at the things that had been disheveled from my wrestling match with Wayne. "I don't want to stay here tonight. I – I can't, Noah. I know it's an imposition, but is there any way I could sleep at the lodge tonight?" She looked so timid and scared, I didn't even hesitate.

"Of course, or you can stay in the cabin if you'd rather."

"Are you sure?" Audrey's voice sounded full of hope.

"Yes, of course," I said, brushing some hair out of her eyes. "Audrey, I never should have broken up with you just because you weren't ready to get married. I was such an ass and I don't blame you if you never forgive me, but that's why I was coming over today. To apologize for pressuring you and to let you know I just want to be with you, whether we're married or not."

"Do you mean it?" Audrey blinked back tears and a huge smile lit up her beautiful face.

I nodded vigorously and said, "I'm sorry about everything, Audrey. Will you take me back?"

"I will!" Audrey threw her arms around my neck and kissed me passionately.

I drove her up to the cabin with two suitcases full of her stuff. Elisa said she didn't mind holding the rest until we were ready to pick it up. The further we got away from the police lights and all the onlookers gossiping about Wayne's arrest, the more Audrey seemed to relax.

"You won't have to worry about him ever again," I tried to reassure her as we entered the cabin and she started looking behind doorways and inside closets. It was an instinct I understood well. Once your life was put in danger, it was hard to lower your guard, but I wanted Audrey to know she didn't have to worry ever again.

She finally collapsed on the couch, exhausted.

"I know he's in jail now, but I can't let go of the fear," she said.

I nodded. "It'll take some time, but you'll get used to it." I sat beside her and wrapped her up in my arms.

"I hope so," she said, her eyes searching mine.

Squeezing her shoulders gently, I said, "He's going away for a long time."

Her face relaxed as I said the words, and I knew it was sinking in that she was finally out of danger. She snuggled up against me.

"And I promise to stay by your side, Audrey, protecting you from whatever dangers life throws at you, for as long as you'll let me."

She looked at me for a long moment, then took my hand.

"Will you be there through good times and bad, through sickness and health, till death do us part?" Audrey asked with a mischievous smile on her sexy lips.

"What are you saying?" I had to be certain before I dared let my heart hope again.

"I was acting out of fear when I turned down your proposal, but I shouldn't have. I'm sorry I reacted that way," she said, and then smiled. "If the offer is still open, I'd love to be your wife, Noah Cole."

"The offer is definitely still open," I said, grinning.

I couldn't believe it! My hands were trembling with excitement as I sprang to my feet, found the ring box I'd carefully put away in a bureau, and fumbled it open. Audrey stood as she watched me.

"Wait, I have to do this right," I said, and went down on one knee in front of her.

"Audrey Sawyer, will you marry me?"

"Yes, Noah Cole, I will."

We were both crying tears of joy as I slipped the ring onto the third finger of her left hand.

Then I kissed her. Gently at first, but the kiss quickly deepened as our arms circled around each other, and we melded together as one.

"My future husband," she said, smiling.

"My future wife." I could hardly believe this was happening, and I couldn't stop grinning.

"Make love to me, Noah," Audrey whispered.

She peeled off her blouse, exposing her stunning breasts to me. I filled my hands with them, and then my mouth, kissing and suckling every inch of her gorgeous flesh.

Quickly, I stripped off all my clothes as she removed the rest of hers, and we lay on the bed together. We'd fucked there countless times, but this was different. This time we were making love for the first time as an engaged couple, and I wanted it to be as beautiful and special as she was.

"I love you so much," Audrey moaned as I spread her thighs and brought my mouth to her most sensitive folds. She clutched at the mattress, arched her back, and writhed with delirious pleasure as I flicked my tongue against her clit one moment, then slowly lapped it the next. Then I took the first two fingers of my left hand and entered her dripping wet slot. Audrey moaned loudly with pleasure and raised her hips, wanting more. Using my tongue and fingers in partnership, I soon had Audrey coming beneath my touch, her voice calling out my name as she reached the zenith of pleasure.

"Now it's my turn," Audrey insisted, and she pushed me down onto the mattress and brought her lips to my rock-hard cock. Audrey expertly made love to me with her mouth, working her magic until I feared I would explode.

"I'm getting too hot," I warned, and Audrey simply smiled.

"In that case, let's cool you off." I watched as she walked naked to the refrigerator and filled a bowl with ice from the freezer.

I gritted my teeth and hissed with painful pleasure as Audrey seductively ran an ice cube over my body, titillating my nipples, trailing down my stomach, and finally torturing the shaft of my cock.

"Is that too cold?" Audrey asked as I winced at the sensation, even as I loved it. "Let me warm you up."

I groaned with ecstasy as Audrey straddled my waist and enveloped my erection with her tight, wet slot. Slowly, she began to thrust, and I could feel the walls of her pussy rippling around me, as she moaned too. Her eyes closed, her head thrown back, and her tits thrust forward. God, she was beautiful!

I wrapped my arms around her torso, pulling her against me, so her tits were pressed against my chest, and her mouth was pressed against mine in a passionate embrace.

We rolled over on the bed and now I was on top, thrusting deep inside her as we kissed and our hands ran over each other's naked bodies. I cupped her breasts as she squeezed my ass, and we tumbled over each other again so now she was on top again, thrusting along the entire length of my erection as I tried to make it last, but I was unable to hold back.

"I'm going to come!" I groaned loudly.

"Me too!" Audrey screamed with ecstasy, and I felt her body spasm as her muscles seized in the throes of her climax. Every neuron in my body exploded with intense pleasure as I orgasmed along with her, clutching her to me as we came together. It was the most powerful orgasm of my life, and the ripples of pleasure pulsed through me even long afterwards, as we lay cuddled together, simply holding each other close.

"I love you so much," I whispered as I caressed her chestnut hair away from her sweaty forehead. "I'm so glad you came back to me."

"I love you too. And I'm so glad you asked me to marry you. I'm just sorry it took me so long to say yes."

"You have nothing to apologize for, Audrey," I said. "I'm the one who should be sorry. I pushed you into accepting my proposal after you'd just come out of an abusive relationship. I get why you hesitated. I never want to make you do anything you don't want to."

"Thanks for saying that," she said. "There's nothing more I want now than to be your wife."

I planted a kiss on her head and traced a finger down the curve of her back.

"So when should we tie the knot?"

She smiled and looked up at me.

"I mean, I don't want to pressure you. We can be engaged as long as you want, even if it's years. However, I'm available as early as tomorrow."

Audrey giggled, then said, "How about we compromise and set the date for six months from now?"

"Sounds good to me," I said, and we made love again.

TWENTY-SEVEN

NOAH

Two months later

"It's a hunting lodge, not a bed and breakfast," I groaned, looking at what Audrey had done to the boarding rooms intended for hunters and fishermen.

"That doesn't mean they can't be beautiful," Audrey insisted. "My mother isn't going to want to stay in a room decorated with antlers, and neither is my sister with her children."

"Do you have to invite your family for the wedding? I didn't invite mine," I joked, but Audrey wasn't laughing.

"You know you can't avoid them forever."

"Your family or mine?" I teased, and this time she did laugh.

"Both." She looked so sexy with her hands on her hips and her lips pursed that I had to kiss her.

The passionate embrace melted away any stubborn hostility either of us may have had, and we ended up on the bed with its floral bedspread, making out.

I never knew it was possible to be this in love with a

woman, and yet every time I looked at Audrey, I loved her even more than I had the moment before. She made me happier than I ever thought I could be, and thanks to the therapist she'd insisted I start going to, I was starting to realize that I was just as worthy of happiness as anybody.

"See? The new bedding's nice, isn't it?" Audrey teased with a sexy smile. "Maybe you should invite your brothers to spend the night here for our wedding, along with my family."

"The bedding is damn nice," I agreed, purposefully ignoring the rest of her comment. It was something I'd discussed with my therapist too, but I just didn't know if I was ready. After all, what right did I have to expect them to come to my wedding?

Yeah, I knew they'd come if I invited them, but I didn't want to obligate them in that way. We weren't close like Audrey's family was. Well, my four brothers were close, but not with me. I was the one black sheep left out on the margins, and it was my own fucking fault. I'd been the one to alienate them all these years. Even after they came up to reconcile with me that one day, I still felt like a stranger among them.

Audrey was always encouraging me to reach out to them, but after everything that happened between us, I just didn't feel like I had earned the right. Maybe I never would.

"Can you go up to the cabin and get that framed photo of me and Mom off the mantel?" Audrey asked. "I want to set it on the nightstand in here for Mom. I think it would be the perfect surprise for her."

"The wedding is still four months away. How soon is she coming to stay?" I asked, trying not to sound freaked out.

Audrey laughed softly, and said, "Relax. She's just

coming for a short vacation. She'll only be here a week, then she's going back home to Charlotte until the wedding. Now please fetch me the photo. I have to remake this bed now that you've messed it up."

"I didn't mess it up as much as I wanted to," I leered playfully, making Audrey giggle as she kissed me again. Fuck, I loved that woman!

I marched back up the trail to get her photo. The sun was already low on the horizon and it was getting hard to see. An animal scampered in the distance, and I turned, expecting to see a hoof or a paw, but all I caught was the remnant of a shadow disappearing into the brush.

I checked the ground with keen eyes, and was startled to see boot tracks. This was no deer or rabbit.

"Who's there?" I shouted out gruffly, but there was no response.

Grabbing my phone, I activated the security system I'd had installed to protect Audrey. The feed from the cabin was black. Someone had disconnected the cameras. Shit!

Instantly on alert, I crept stealthily towards the cabin. It couldn't be a saboteur from Save the Salamanders. Ever since Paul had been hired to run the preservation department of Pine Creek Lodge, the animal rights group had praised us as innovative heroes and we hadn't had any trouble from them. So, who had cut the camera feed? Could it be Wayne? Had he been let out of prison on some technicality, or even escaped?

My heart was pounding in my fucking chest as all my senses went on high alert, searching for danger.

The lights were on in my cabin and I saw the silhouette of a man cross by before the lights switched off and the cabin went dark, but I wasn't fooled. Whoever was in there was still there, lurking in the dark, waiting to pounce on me or Audrey when we came home. Well, they were in for a deadly surprise.

I kicked open the door and shouted out loudly, "I've got you, asshole! Get down on the floor, right fucking now!"

"Is that any way to greet family? How about a hug instead?" a cheerful voice called out, and my jaw dropped in shock. It was Ethan!

As he wrapped his arms around me in a brotherly hug, I felt all the stress and fear leave my body.

"All right, my turn, asshole." It was Owen, followed by Gavin and Jared. All four of my brothers were there, each hugging me in turn. I had to blink back tears of emotion at seeing them all.

"You guys scared the shit out of me. What the hell are you doing here?" I chuckled happily.

"You didn't think you could get away with not having us throw an engagement party for our brother, did you?" Ethan asked, ruffling the top of my head.

"That's why I never told you guys I was engaged," I joked, trying to hide how embarrassed I felt that I hadn't.

"Well, in a town as small as North Haven, you didn't have to. We found out anyway, and started planning this. Audrey helped us out by distracting you and getting you out of the cabin. Sean turned off the security cameras, and we did the rest."

I looked around and discovered there was beer, a full buffet of appetizers, and Jared pushed play on his iPod to get the music started. A few minutes later, Audrey showed up with my sisters-in-law. We were all packed tight in my tiny cabin, but somehow it felt cozy and not the least bit crowded.

"You did this," I accused Audrey as I drew her to me and kissed her lovingly.

"Not me. Your brothers planned the whole thing."

"But you knew about it and didn't say a word," I glowered at her playfully.

"Ethan said I was going to be part of the Cole family and that meant playing pranks on each other. What choice did I have but to play along?"

"Well, I'm glad you did," I said gratefully.

The party lasted for hours, and I was relieved to see how well Audrey fit in. She was more of a Cole than I was, which wasn't that hard. My brothers, however, made it easy for me to come back into the fold, bearing no grudges, and picking right back up where we left off with inside jokes and brotherly roughhousing.

"Are they always like this?" Audrey gaped as Jared challenged Owen to an ax-throwing contest in the front yard, and nearly decapitated Gavin when the handle slipped from his grip.

"I'm afraid so, but you'll get used to it," Gavin's wife, Jolie, said, making Audrey laugh. Then she leaned in close to my ear and whispered, "So will you. Your brothers have really missed you. It's good to have you back in the family."

After that night, I couldn't get rid of my brothers. They were up at the lodge constantly, helping with wedding plans, giving unwanted advice, or just shooting the bull. It felt good, better than I ever imagined it would, and I had Audrey to thank for it.

She'd changed my life for the better in every possible way, and I loved her more than I ever thought possible. The best part was our lives together were just beginning.

EPILOGUE

AUDREY

"You look stunning, Audrey!"

Mom cried tears of joy as she straightened my veil. It had belonged to my grandmother, and the little silk flowers at the crown were yellowed and frail, but I wanted to wear it anyway, so Noah had paid a fortune to have it restored. Whatever the cost, it was worth it, as the veil crested with tiny white roses gleamed like a crown atop my head, and I felt like a true princess.

My trumpet-style gown was adorned with beads that sparkled like a million stars. The shape of it hugged my every curve like it had been poured over me, and I'd never felt more elegant.

"Thanks, Mom," I said, trying not to cry myself. I was so glad she was here.

The music began to play, and the usher took my mother down the aisle, followed by my bridesmaids. Elisa served as my maid of honor, and looked wonderful in a gown of pale pink. The flower girl, Maisy, was the last to go, eagerly tossing rose petals at the guests with her usual flair, nearly making her the star of the show.

Then the music changed, and "Here Comes the Bride" sounded through the air. This was it! It was my turn to go.

"You look beautiful, pumpkin." My dad hugged me tight, before crooking his arm and placing my hand upon it. "I'm just glad you've found someone who'll make you happy."

"Thanks, Dad. I truly believe he'll make all my dreams true," I said, and meant it.

With that, my father led me down the aisle, where Noah was waiting, looking incredible in his military dress uniform. The whole audience rose to their feet as I passed by, but all I could see was Noah, gazing back at me with all the love he felt for me reflected in his eyes.

The ceremony went by in a daze as I put all my effort into not crying on the altar. Then, suddenly, the preacher announced, "I now pronounce you man and wife. You may kiss the bride."

The crowd cheered as Noah pulled me to him and kissed me with such fiery passion, it stole my breath away. Not to be outdone, I kissed him back just as romantically, until the preacher had to practically break us apart.

Then, it was time to party. The reception was everything I wanted it to be. I got to dance with my dad to our favorite song, and poor Noah had to dance with my mother, but he handled it with grace. When it was time to toss the bouquet, I aimed right for Elisa, but somehow the bouquet of roses landed right in Lauren's hands, making the whole crowd laugh as the feisty cougar blushed. Then it was time for Noah to remove my garter, and he handed it right to his brother Jared.

"It looks like you're the only Cole left unattached, so you're next," Noah teased, and the rest of his brothers took turns ruffling his hair and giving him a hard time, but it was all in good fun. Even Jared couldn't stop laughing, insisting that he'd be a carefree bachelor forever.

Then, at long last, the limo came to pick me and Noah up and take us away from the noise and the crowd, away on our honeymoon.

"I told you it was a mistake to invite all my brothers to our wedding," Noah teased, but it was obvious from the light dancing in his eyes that he was happy they'd all come to support him.

"I don't know about that. I kinda thought today was perfect," I said.

"Don't you want to know where I'm taking you for our honeymoon?" Noah taunted. He'd been torturing me for weeks with hints, but never would say. It was a game we both enjoyed, especially before and after making love.

"Actually, I don't care anymore," I said haughtily, looking out the window with feigned disinterest. Truthfully, I was dying to know.

"Oh, really? So you don't care to know that we'll be spending three weeks lounging by the pool of a luxury spa?" Noah said. I gasped and turned to look at him so I could see if he was serious. "They have cement Jacuzzis, artificial jungles, and even a manmade waterfall. What do you think?"

Noah's eyes were all lit up, and I hated to dampen his enthusiasm. Plastering a fake smile on my face, I said, "I'm sure we'll have a great time, especially if we're together."

"What's wrong?" Noah frowned. He knew me too well for me to try to hide my disappointment.

"It's just the idea of artificial flowers and fake waterfalls. I guess I've been spoiled living in our beautiful forest. Nothing ever compares to nature in its true form."

"I knew you'd say that!" Noah laughed, his face full of

joy. "I was just kidding about the resort. I'm taking you to Alaska for a month. We'll hike through Denali National Park and sail around the Kenai Fjords, we could see grizzly bears or sea lions, and I've even scheduled a special helicopter tour of a glacier."

"Now that's a honeymoon!" I threw myself at Noah, kissing him excitedly.

It would be the adventure of a lifetime.

When I first moved to North Haven, it had felt like a place where dreams came true. I just never imagined that it would be this wonderful.

With Noah by my side, I was truly getting my happily ever after.

If you liked this book, you'll LOVE **Faking It with My Best Friend!**

It's the story of pro pitcher Jared Cole and feisty redhead Fiona. Fans of fake engagements and friends-to-lovers romance will fall in love with this standalone!

Fake engaged to my best friend, the hot baseball star.
Kill me now.

Jared Cole needs a fake fiancée to fix his broken reputation and save his career.
Easy.
That's what friends are for.

Except...

No one told me on-camera cuddles and shared hotel beds were part of the deal.

And I didn't expect Jared to look at me like I'm the only woman in the world.

I can't fall for him.

This is all pretend, right?

But then he kisses me when no one's looking.

Things are about to get *very* real.

Grab your copy of **Faking It with My Best Friend** now!

SNEAK PEEK: FAKING IT WITH MY BEST FRIEND

JARED

"You guys hitting the club tonight?"

I tried to keep my voice light as I entered the locker room with my teammates.

Tense silence hung in the air for too long. I cringed.

The guys were pissed off at me, but I couldn't blame them. We'd lost the game. I'd let them all down.

Finally, Marcos, the first baseman, piped up.

"Hell, yeah!" he hollered.

And just like that, the dark cloud in the locker room lifted. To my surprise, the rest of the guys cheered.

The team had gone from feeling defeated to whooping and howling in a matter of seconds. A couple of guys playfully slapped me on the back as they headed for the showers.

"Don't beat yourself up, Jared," one of them said to me. "We were all off our game tonight."

"We'll kick ass next season," the other said.

But their words didn't lift the heavy disappointment weighing me down.

I knew I'd fucked up. There was no denying it — we'd

lost the most important game of the season, and it was my fault.

I stood in the shower for a long time. With my head hung low, I let the hot water pour over my aching shoulder, trying to wash away the frustration that consumed me.

Baseball meant everything to me.

I'd spent my whole life working to get here – pitching for a professional team. Up until tonight, we'd had a great season. We'd even had a shot at the league championship. *Everyone* knew it. All our hard work was finally paying off.

Life couldn't have gotten any better than that.

And then my fucking shoulder went out.

I tried to play through the pain, but it just kept getting worse. Tonight had been the final game to determine if the Kestrels would make it to the playoffs. Everything had been riding on this.

Thanks to me, we had lost.

I felt like complete shit. I'd played great all season, and then when it really counted, I blew it.

The shower did nothing to wash away my pain, physically or mentally. What I needed was to get fucking wasted in the club tonight. There was nothing like a night of fun to help a man forget his troubles.

"Now that our season is over, it's time to party. Let's get this vacation started right. First round is on me!" I called out with a rowdy whoop as I got dressed, trying to lift my mood with fake enthusiasm. The locker room exploded with wolf howls and rambunctious cheers.

I couldn't wait to drown my sorrows in one of Boston's finest nightclubs. I needed to take my mind off the game. I knew the other guys felt the same way.

Suddenly, the guys went silent as our head coach

entered the room, looking grim. Of course, the bald fifty-two-year-old always looked that way.

He focused his beady gaze right at me and barked, "Jared Cole, the party will have to wait. Get your ass in my office, now."

"Sure thing, Coach," I answered. My mouth turned dry as I watched him turn and leave the room.

"Ooh. You're in deep shit," Marcos said.

My friend couldn't resist giving me a hard time, but it was all in fun. My teammates had become more of a family to me than my actual brothers. My real family back in Virginia was always pressuring me to grow up and settle down. They wanted me to get married, move back home and start a family, but that wasn't me. My teammates understood that and let me be my true self, carefree and enjoying the prime of my life.

"Fuck you, Marcos," I shot back.

We both laughed, but inside my mind was reeling. What did Coach Hawkins want to talk to me about? Sure, we'd lost tonight, but overall we'd had a great season. My pitching had brought this team almost to the playoffs, and if my shoulder hadn't given out, we'd have won today. This must be about something more personal.

Shit!

I swallowed hard as it hit me.

He must have seen the viral video of me partying with some friends at the club last week – Natalia and Inga.

I'd had a little too much to drink. I think I must have passed out, because I never would have let them record me and post it online, and I certainly wouldn't have let them do drugs around me. I never touched narcotics – that was a guaranteed way to get kicked off the team.

The video made it look like I had gotten high and had a

threesome with those women before I'd passed out. But it wasn't true. I just had to convince Coach Hawkins of my innocence.

As I entered the coach's office ready to defend myself, I was startled to see the room full of people. The team physician was there, Dr. Barrett, along with my Public Relations Agent, Nicolette Raiyn, and most ominously of all, the team manager himself, Mr. Walter Douglas.

A knot tightened in my gut.

"Jared, please have a seat," Coach said, and I couldn't help but notice there wasn't a smile in the room. Shit. They were taking this viral video more seriously than I feared.

"Listen, Coach," I started nervously. "I know that video makes things look bad, but I was only drinking shots that night, I swear."

"Save it, Jared," Coach said, stopping my speech cold. "Dr. Barrett has the diagnosis for your shoulder injury, and I thought we should all hear it together."

The doctor gave it to me straight, and for once I wished he'd tried to sugar coat it a little. The diagnosis was far worse than I'd feared. I had a torn rotator cuff.

It was quite possibly a career-ending injury. From the mournful look on all their faces, I could tell they were about to cut me from the team, but I refused to let them.

"I can recover from this," I stated emphatically. My fucking life's career was on the line. I had to convince them all I could do this. "There's a terrific physical therapist in my hometown. My brother's a doctor, and he highly recommended him. I know if I work hard on rehabbing this injury, I'll be ready to play again by the time training camp starts in the spring."

"I don't know, Jared. It's a pretty serious injury. You've had a good run with the Kestrels. Maybe it's time you consider finding that next passion in life," Coach said gently.

I wiped a line of sweat from my forehead.

"There *is* no other passion. My whole life, all I've ever wanted is to play baseball," I insisted, perhaps a little too forcefully. Struggling to sound calm, I said levelly, "I can do this. Just give me a chance to prove it. I'll work my ass off. I'll do whatever the physical therapist tells me to do. By spring, my pitching arm will be fully recovered, I promise. If not, then you can cut me from the team. But don't do it without giving me this chance to prove myself."

The men pulled together in a little huddle, whispering among themselves, but Nicolette just leaned back in her chair and crossed her long legs. Twisting a tendril of her platinum blonde hair around her finger, she looked at me.

"A torn rotator cuff isn't the only thing you need to recover from."

"What are you talking about?" I blinked, and in response she held up her phone. On the screen was an image of the viral video. She scrolled to an article calling me the 'Playboy Pitcher,' and then a meme, followed by another and then another. It seemed like everyone on social media was talking about that damn video of me partying. I was fucked.

"You've got an image problem," Nicolette stated matter-of-factly. "Even before this video went viral, you'd developed an image as a bad boy who likes to party at the clubs, sleeping with a different girl every night, sometimes more than one. We've lost a sponsor because of you, Jared."

I glanced at the manager, who shook his head in frustration. That *couldn't* be good.

"Baseball is a sport for families to watch together," Nicolette continued. "Parents want to bring their kids to the stadium so they can see the players they admire. Maybe even get an autographed ball. Do you think any parent out there wants their kid to have a ball right now autographed by this guy?"

She held up a screen shot of me passed out drunk on the bar while my friends from the club did drugs all around me. I felt my skin burn with humiliation.

"I'll fix that too," I stated with determination, my fists clenched.

"Really? How?" Nicolette demanded. She was in charge of PR, not just for me, but for the entire team, so when one of us fucked up, it damaged the reputation for the entire Kestrels organization. I knew this could be as deadly to my career as my torn rotator cuff.

"I'll change my image," I insisted, running a hand through my hair as my mind raced. "By the time spring training begins, I'll no longer be known as a playboy. I come from a small town in Virginia, with picket fences and home-made apple pie. I'll spend the off-season there. I'll be the picture of all-American wholesomeness. Just watch and see."

"Yeah, right! Now all you need is a wife and a golden retriever!" the manager said. He and Coach laughed together heartily.

Coach clasped me on the back and said, "Who are you going to get to play the wife?"

Nicolette lit up at the idea. "You know, it's too bad Jared can't come back from that small town married, or at least engaged," she said. "If only he could be reformed by falling back in love with an old high school sweetheart, it would really do a lot to turn his image around. The public eats that kind of thing up."

The idea put a sour taste in my mouth. My high school sweetheart, Casey, had cheated on me and left me brokenhearted. Only my best friend had helped me through that dark and terrible time. She'd stood by my side, supporting me. And she encouraged me to go after my dream of playing baseball.

Shit! That was it! Suddenly, I brightened with the idea.

My best friend, Fiona Hawthorne.

I was certain she would help me if I asked. After all, we had been best friends for most of my childhood. Back then, there was nothing we wouldn't do for each other, and this was definitely my hour of need.

"What if I can make that happen?" I said aloud.

Suddenly, all eyes turned on me.

I showed them a picture of Fiona and told them of my idea to get engaged to her – for pretend. Then, after the baseball season had begun, we could quietly and amicably 'break up.' By then, my shoulder and my reputation would be fully healed.

"I'll assist with photo opportunities, interviews, and presenting the best images of you and your new fiancée to the public," Nicolette offered, clearly loving the idea.

"I'll contact your doctor and the physical therapist in North Haven to set up your first appointment," Dr. Barrett said, letting me know he was on board too.

Now it was just up to Coach and the team manager, Mr. Douglas.

My heart pounded in my chest. My whole life was in their hands. If they decided to just cut me from the team right then, I'd be dead at the age of twenty-seven, with no future ahead of me.

Despite the gravity of the moment, I refused to beg anymore, and waited for my fate with dignity. I'd stated my case, and now it was up to them.

Finally, Mr. Douglas gave a slight nod to Coach.

"All right, Jared," Mr. Douglas said. "Go home to North Haven. Do whatever you have to do in physical therapy to get that rotator cuff healed, and give this fake fiancée thing a try. Maybe you can clean up this social media mess you've made. If you succeed at both, you can stay on the team. If you fail at either one, you're finished."

The knot in my stomach loosened as relief washed over me.

"Thank you, you won't regret it," I said, grinning and shaking their hands.

But my happiness didn't last long. As soon as I strode out of the office, a heavy cloud settled over me.

I hadn't seen Fiona since I'd hugged her goodbye when I left for college. That was nearly nine whole years ago. Since then we'd kept in touch via email or text, but nothing more. Would she really say yes to doing such a huge favor for me?

Even if she agreed to the idea, would we really be able to convince the public we were in love?

Maybe I was getting us into something too crazy to pull off.

The Fiona I knew when we were young could do anything. I just hoped she could help save my career.

Grab your copy of **Faking It with My Best Friend** now!

Printed in Great Britain
by Amazon

37234788R00116